AS IF I AM NOT THERE

Alexandra Filia

AS IF I AM NOT THERE

DEDICATION

In Loving Memory of My Sister Eleni.
She would've got an enormous kick out of this book.

Watch me shrink.
I'll prove it to everyone.
I won't stop until I'm tiny.
I will be thin.

CONTENTS

Chapter One

Happy

I love my name, Gwyneth. In Welsh it means *blessed* or *happy*, which is exactly the way I'm feeling today. School is out, I am thin, and we are about to go on vacation. I think my name suits me. I am generally a happy person and take most things in stride. When I was a little girl, my mom used to call me her ray of sunshine. Most kids don't remember much from when they were little, but I do. My childhood was magical and full of love and hugs.

Gwyneth is my grandmother's name, except she was *Winny* all her life, Mamgu Winny to us. I'm not sure when we started calling her Mamgu (which is grandma in old Welsh), but I suppose Mom suggested it to avoid confusion, since she and I share the same name. I grew up as *Winny*, or *Gwinny*, meaning *annoying* according to my sister Ella.

Last year, my first year in Upper School, I reinvented myself as *Gwyneth*. You can tell how long people have known me by what they call me. In my immediate family, confusion reigns. I am *Winny*, *Gigi*, and *Gwen* in the first person and when all is well. When I am spoken of in the third person, or if I have done something wrong, it is always *Gwyneth*.

"*Gwyneth* will not be coming out tonight because *Gwyneth* has not finished her homework." "*Winny*, give me a hand putting away the shopping." "*Gwyneth*, how many times have I asked you to set the table?"

You get the idea. I have given up correcting my family and respond to every variation they shout out, but at school I'm very strict and will pretend not to have heard unless *Gwyneth* is used. One has to draw the line somewhere if they want a new name to stick.

Names are so interesting. A name is at the centre of who we are. Names define us, and yet, unlike hair, weight, or even eye colour and other personal characteristics, it is the one thing we change the least often. Sure, we have nicknames, but rarely any wholesale change. People tend to stick to the name they were given at birth. They hope that the next generation will also be given that name, no matter how unattractive or old fashioned it may be. Have you ever wondered how Gertrude survived as a name choice?

So, the question is: Does our name define us? What about last names? I was born *Stokes*. Stokes is my family name, our collective achievements and triumphs, our beliefs, the name we must honour, not something to be given up lightly. I have already decided I will be Stokes first, and whatever my future husband's name is, second. Ella and I are the last of the line. If we give up Stokes, there will be no more Stokes. It feels a bit like a betrayal.

And then, one has to wonder, Winny or Gwyneth? Do names have the power to change how we feel about ourselves?

Winny Stokes was a hardworking ten-year-old full of imagination and wonder. Gwyneth Stokes is a confident young woman, ready to take on the world. Gwyneth Stokes future husband's name will be a compromise—a salute to the past and a wave to the future.

As you probably guessed, I am almost seventeen. I am 174 cm and the third tallest in my class. My hair is a fiery red that runs in our family. At the moment it is quite long, almost to my waist, but I have been thinking about cutting it off to mark my new status as an Upper School girl.

I love my hair. It is sort of a trademark. A great head of hair, if I may say so myself. It's thick, long, and really curly—big flowing ringlets. Not to sound like I'm bragging, but it's distinctive, memorable. It totally matches my spontaneous, goofy, crazy personality.

Being in Upper School means no more uniform, and I am super excited about being able to wear stylish clothes to school every day. When school finished last week, I wanted to throw out my uniform like my friends did, but Mom insisted I keep it for Ella, because we have to be careful with money, which I hate. I reminded Mom that there is no possible way Ella would ever fit into my size six uniform, but there was no talking her out of it.

Speaking of weight, I am looking quite good at the moment. I have managed to shed the GCSE weight and I am down to 52kg. I have been battling my weight all my life, ever since I was a little girl. Fat, then thin, then fat, then thin, and so on.

Every morning when I wake up, my first thoughts are: *Did I eat too much yesterday? What is the scale going to show? How many hours of exercise will counteract that*

9

extra helping of spaghetti Bolognese? Will my clothes feel too tight or too loose?

I can't tell you how often I have heard from my aunties and others in my family that I'd be really pretty if I lost some weight. I don't disagree, but it really hurts to hear, even though they are right.

The main problem is that when I gain weight it all goes to my cheeks and neck and I end up looking like a hamster who just ate its whole supply of nuts in one go. I don't look anything like these very attractive overweight models with the stunning faces. Even though Ella is fat, she looks better than me as a fat person. I am ultra-conscious of this, so I am perpetually on a diet.

One kilo down can make me so happy that in the middle of any catastrophe I can keep my wits about me because AT LEAST I AM NOT FAT! You think I'm exaggerating? When I was eleven and Ella was eight, she was rushed to hospital with something serious. I remember very clearly taking the bus with Mom to the hospital. I remember what I was wearing, and I also remember my overriding thoughts at the time. *I look good in these black trousers. I can't believe they fit. This new diet is really working. I hope Ella is okay.* It must have been serious enough for her to be rushed into hospital, but for the life of me I can't remember any specifics about the incident.

What is puzzling is that I don't remember at all what the emergency was.

Chapter Two

Eating Marathons

Others do running marathons. I do eating marathons—and without exception, I regret it as soon as I cross the finish line. My eating is not on schedule. I can go all day eating nothing, but the minute I'm not busy I get ravenously hungry. I can eat and eat and eat non-stop. I'm an early riser, so 6 a.m. is as late as I ever stay in bed. From 6 a.m. onwards I can go all day and not have a single bite of food. I don't even get hungry. Then when I get home at 4 p.m. I collapse on the sofa with all my energy gone. Suddenly, I'll remember I'm hungry.

Here is the pattern. First, I will have a few carrots. Then I will jump on the bananas (honestly, I can eat seven in a row). Unsatisfied, I will eat any bread that is lying around the house, along with a slice of cheese. Having had one slice of cheese, I may have a couple more (in for a penny, in for a pound). When dinner comes around, I will be very good. I won't touch the carbs or any sauces and will choose chicken with salad or an omelet, or even baked beans with tuna. While doing my homework, there will undoubtedly be chocolate and possibly a handful of popcorn. By bedtime, as I look back upon my day of eating, I'll be totally disgusted with my eating marathon and I'll go to bed swearing the next day will be different.

For those of you who are good at calorie counting, you are looking at over 2,500 packed into a few evening hours. I work out a lot, so I burn about 500 extra calories doing an exercise class or a 5K run. This means that in terms of weight I stand still, and the three kilos I want to lose are my permanent buddies. If you have a lot of weight to lose, you may be sniggering at this moment and mumbling under your breath that I am another annoying girl pointlessly complaining about a few extra kilos. But this is very far from the truth. I was once a fat girl, obsessed with food and exercising, pedaling really hard just to maintain a stable weight.

There is, of course, a secret solution for getting rid of all those calories, but for years I found it impossible to do. Many of my friends could enjoy mountains of crisps and chocolate and then effortlessly stick a finger down their throats and get rid of the guilty binges before they became saddlebags. I would sit next to the toilet bowl admiring their technique and waiting my turn, but I just couldn't persevere. At the first sign of retching, I would withdraw the offending finger and hopelessly resign myself to a few extra hours at the gym to get rid of the calories.

Last year, I finally got the hang of it thanks to my friend Ginny and a toothbrush, and I was over the moon. I can eat anything I want, and it doesn't matter. My friend Louise has a second secret to losing weight. She buys pills that make you go to the bathroom. You can get them over the counter, and they make you lose lots of weight and feel light as a feather. I take them once in a while, but I don't really like the sharp stomach pain that you have to endure when they start to work.

I'm not sure how it is for other people, but I think about food and weight at least once an hour, or perhaps at some level, all the time. I am always in touch with how my clothes feel, and I mentally calculate calories and fat content several times a day—and not just at mealtimes. I think I have a special part of my brain which is dedicated exclusively to weight. I plan my meals carefully and often skip a meal if on the previous day I had gone off the rails eating.

My biggest worry in life is that I will get fat (again). I have been fat a few times, and it is a terrible feeling, especially as the sizes go up, and little by little I give up on the clothes which get tighter and tighter. During my fat periods, I assume I weigh around 64-65kg. I say "assume" because I can't even bring myself to look at the number on the scales. I just want to be thin again. When this happens, I look at old photos. And damn, I miss that body. Usually this gets me in gear, but sometimes I can languish at this weight for months, too demotivated to do anything about it.

Unfortunately, I have a very large wardrobe. I keep all the clothes which don't fit, because I know they will eventually fit me on the way up or on the way down. My friends are always on some sort of diet as well, so perhaps I am not the only one who worries about it all the time. I don't think I have an eating disorder though, because I've never thrown up and I don't really eat much junk. I don't in any way identify with the pictures of those girls I see in magazines—

you know, the ones with their bones sticking out like concentration camp victims.

Everyone on both sides of my family are good eaters, except for one far-removed cousin who, according to Mamgu Winny, was seriously anorexic. She lived to be quite old but always looked like a skeleton. But that is really far in the past. Maybe she had another kind of sickness which kept her skinny. Who knows?

I am also a fitness fanatic. Always have been. I run and I lift weights at the gym. I know that as long as I don't give up on my exercise, I will always be motivated to go back on my diet. It is hard not to when I know that to burn off a single piece of toast, I need to run for ten minutes. Three pieces of toast or a bagel is a full 5K run. Totally not worth it, right? So why do I do it? I don't know. It's like, every night when I get back from school, I totally give up on myself. The minute I sit in front of my homework, all of a sudden I have intense munchies, and nothing fills the void but food. I just have to keep eating. To avoid becoming a hippo, I eat super slowly and mostly healthy foods.

I eat as I work, so my computer keyboard is gross and covered in seeds and spit. I cleaned it the other day so I don't get cholera, although cholera may be exactly what I need to stop eating. If not cholera, at least gastroenteritis. I got that last year and I lost five kilos. Even in the darkest day of the gastro, when I was puking and pooping everywhere, in the back of my mind I was happy and content, because after every puke or poop I would get on the scale and mark my progress. I wonder if anyone else does that when they are sick, or if I have a special kind of twisted thinking when it comes to eating and dieting?

I think not. Being thin is very important. Everybody knows that. Mom says that a guy will overlook an ugly face but not a fat body. In all my romance novels, there is never a fat heroine or even a stout one. They are all ethereal, barely-there skinny maidens. Also, I think any guy would be super embarrassed to take a fat girl to a party or out to meet his friends. I have been to many parties but have never seen a guy ask a fat girl to dance.

Secretly, I think some guys like fat girls—but not for dating, just for sex. I have seen the mags at the newsagent, and someone must be buying them. Even in our neighbourhood we must have some secret fat-girl lovers, because every week behind the modesty curtain there are new issues of *Plumpers* and *Big Butt*.

Even my dad is anti-fat, even though he has gained a lot of weight since I was little. When I was at my fattest, he flat out told me I was approaching the perfect shape of the ancient Greeks which, he said, was the sphere. I could tell that there was disappointment behind his comment. And wow, it really hurt. Of course he doesn't want a fat daughter. Who does? I wonder how he feels about the rest of his fat family. Ella has been piling on the kilos, and so has Mom.

My plan is to be the saving grace of this family. I have visions of having a tiny waist, flat abs, a thigh gap, and not an ounce of extra fat anywhere. Perhaps I should swallow a tapeworm. I wonder if this works or if it would make me really sick? There is no conclusive evidence on the online diet forums—and yes, they exist—but I wouldn't know where to get one, anyway.

Everybody likes thin. This is clear. I don't agree with fat-shaming, but I'm also very much against me being fat. I can see why fat girls want the world to think it's okay to be fat, but I also know that if they had a bit of self-control they would all prefer to be thin. They just can't be bothered to control what they eat. I feel a bit disloyal and mean to Ella and Mom when I think this, but seriously, I have watched them both eat junk and take second and third helpings of unhealthy food at dinner time.

I think our family is unusual in that Mom is so worried about us being fat, but at the same time feeds us and herself all the time. She tells us not to eat bread, but there is always fresh bread on the table. Mom says the bread is for Dad, who is a man and works hard, but I know she is the one who loves bread and can eat half a loaf while sitting at the dinner table.

It is so hard to stay thin at our house, even though all of us are talking about food and dieting almost every day.

Chapter Three

Hillside Row

We live in a beautiful four-bedroom house on Hillside Row which has been in the family for generations. It was built by my great grandfather, Thomas Sr., in the early 1900s. By 1929, he had gone from being a penniless apprentice to owning two successful shops of his own. He used his money to buy land in what was at that time the outskirts of town. He built the family home halfway up what is affectionately called the *Mountain of Heaven*, proudly standing tall at 149 metres. There, he built what can only be described as a family compound to house his expanding brood of five children, assorted nephews, cousins, and aunties. The *Mountain of Heaven* is now in the centre of our town, but in 1929 it bordered a beautiful forest where my grandad and great uncles would go hunting for rabbits and other small game. As the town grew, houses were built on either side of what became Hillside Row.

Hillside Row is impossibly steep—so steep, in fact, that in the late 1980s the council finally closed it to traffic and planted wild orange trees in evenly-spaced rows. When my mom and dad married and moved to the family compound in 1985, Hillside Row was a steep, unpaved dirt road with steps running down both sides. Whenever it rained, the street turned into a vicious torrent of mud cascading all the way down to Lyndhurst Avenue.

My neighbourhood is a giant playground. The Johnsons and their daughter Rosie—who is one of my best friends in the world—live right across the street. She has twin younger brothers called Finn and Jeremy, who are Ella's age. Their favourite game is war. They often drag Rosie and me into the game, even though we are almost *marriageable age*, as Mamgu Winny points out every time she wants us to do adult chores. When we are not trying to poke each other's eye out with spit balls in blow tubes, we do each other's makeup and paint our nails in Rosie's pink bedroom. She is so lucky! For her sixteenth birthday, her mom let her turn her whole bedroom pink. Other than the white carpet, everything else is some shade of pink.

The house next to ours is an up-and-down duplex. Aunt Sophie lives in the bottom flat. She's not our real aunt, but we are close to her and have been calling her that since we were little. Sophie's husband works at Mamgu Winny's shop and has worked there since he was eighteen. They have two boys who are much older than we are. George is an electrician's apprentice and Phil makes awnings. Both boys live at home and share a tiny room. Aunt Sophie helps Mom with household chores. When we were little, she would babysit us and feed us French fries which she made from scratch. I asked my parents if she was our slave and I am embarrassed to this day about my ignorance. They are lovely people and have been a huge help to our family. Phil even made an awning for our garden and refused to take any money in return.

In the mid-1990s, Hillside Row was finally paved. Little ridges were imprinted in the cement to help the ambitious drivers who tried to go up or down. Most of them failed to make any headway on the way up, and very rarely did anyone attempt the steep downhill plunge. Despite the ridges, Hillside Row remains treacherous for cars and pedestrians alike. It is not unusual to see women walking down Hillside Row in their bare feet, holding their heels in one hand, having been caught unawares by the slippery steepness of our street. My mom keeps a pair of rubber-sole slip-ons by the kitchen door for anyone who needs to navigate the way down the hill to the newsagent. Ella and I use them every day when we are sent to get milk, the Times, and the occasional ice cream when Mamgu Winny is in a good mood.

Our newsagent is almost a family friend. Mom has an informal credit line at his shop, and we are allowed to buy things such as comic books and sweets and he'll add them to the weekly bill. Of course, I don't buy sweets anymore, but I do buy lots of diet soda and the occasional Marie Claire or Glamour magazine, especially if they have a sample. Sometimes the bill gets too high and we are banned from buying anything for a few weeks, but things soon return to normal.

I really love our neighbourhood and I hope I get to live here forever. I know almost everyone. Plus, we have the biggest house on the street, which makes me feel very important.

It's silly, but I like it.

Chapter Four

Mamgu Winny

Mamgu Winny lives with us in the granny flat. Her apartment has a separate entrance, but she never uses it, preferring to come in and out of the door which connects to the main house. She is Dad's mom and has lived in the house all her life. She carries her extra pounds gracefully, and zooms around the house, setting an elaborate dinner table with her shaking left hand, a remnant of her brain aneurysm operation. She used to be a piano teacher, but now she can't play anymore, which is a real shame.

Even so, her piano still dominates the living room, and a man comes in once a year to tune it, though no one else in the house plays either. It is a beautiful instrument which was given to her by her dad in 1950 as a graduation present. It arrived from Germany in a giant container and has been in the same spot since that day. Mamgu Winny used to practice every day before her aneurysm. She took the French doors off their hinges because she believes everything should be open. When she studied, we could all hear the endless repetition of each musical phrase as she struggled to get them perfect. Once, when I was ten, I opened the back of the piano and threw an egg onto the keys. The tuner had to come twice that year, and nobody was particularly amused. The relentless practice stopped for a couple of weeks. Now that Mamgu Winny can't play anymore, I miss it and wish I had never been so mean.

Mamgu Winny and Mom argue all the time over the most trivial of things, such as leaving the lights on or filling the fridge with leftovers, which appears to be Mamgu Winny's favourite pastime. Even though she is at least ten years past retirement, she still goes to work every day from 8 a.m. to 3 p.m. She manages a shop of painting and decorating supplies which was left to her when granddad died. The shop makes zero money, and Dad has tried more than once to get her to close it down, but she will hear none of it. Every morning, Mom has to drive her to the centre of town and help her lift the heavy green shutters.

At 3 p.m. she drives back and together they close the shop.

Chapter Five

Mom

Mom rarely walks anywhere, preferring to take the car, even to go to the nearby newsagent. Her car is a story in itself—full of dings, nicks, and scratches on the outside with shoes and jackets in a jumble on the backseat. More than once she's forgotten to renew her insurance, run out of gas, or added to her collection of unpaid parking tickets. It's a bit of a joke in the neighbourhood, the way she parks her little grey car on pavements directly in front of "no parking" signs. No spot is too small for her. She will not hesitate to make it bigger by gently bumping her way in.

Mom is warm and funny, short and round. She is only 150cm tall and appears to roll rather than walk when she is in a hurry. Her door is open to friends and family and there is always something delicious cooking in the oven. My friends love coming over to our house to talk to my mom, even when I'm not there. She has answers to every teenage problem in the world and dishes out her good advice together with an endless stream of snacks. Unlike my friends, I am unwilling to take either the advice or the food. Who listens to their mom anyway?

Our kitchen is chaotic and colourful, with a big table in the middle and loads of stuff on every surface. Mom wears thick, tinted glasses on top of her head when she tries to make out a recipe or the small letters on the back of a bottle. She is nearly blind, but for years she pretended she didn't need glasses. She finally gave up and got glasses when I was born because, as she told us, she couldn't always tell which part of the baby needed feeding and which needed changing.

Mom is forever looking for her bag, her keys, or her glasses. She runs around the house mumbling, "Who took my keys?" or "I put my bag right here at the table. Who moved it?" Her bag is always hanging behind the kitchen door, her glasses are almost always on her head, and as for the keys . . . they could be anywhere. She regularly locks herself out of the house or her car, which is why our kitchen door is always unlocked. Anyone can walk in, day or night, and it drives Dad crazy.

Mamgu Winny locks her own flat door, claiming she is not prepared to be robbed and even raped—to which we all laugh as we try to imagine the kind of thief who would want one of her frilly nighties or her many pairs of slippers. Mamgu Winny does not believe in having many possessions, and to the dismay of her now long-deceased husband, she kept giving away her jewellery to her friends, and even to the many maids she had when she first got married. All she has left is an amethyst ring she always wears. She will not say where it came from or the story behind it, and because of that, we all suspect she had some sort of secret affair.

There is something in Mamgu Winny's flat we all want to get our hands on someday—a box of letters she keeps on the top shelf of her wardrobe. Dad told us that his mom had many admirers as a young lady. In fact, she had one husband and two fiancés before she met my grandfather.

The letters apparently tell the whole story. In the box, there is also all the secret correspondence with the mysterious Andrew, a man who loved Mamgu Winny passionately. Up until the day he died, he always called Mamgu Winny on her birthday. One day, when Mamgu Winny was out for the day, Ella and I found the door unlocked and snuck into her flat. The first box we opened was nothing more than a very elaborate sewing kit, with all the shoulder pads Mamgu Winny always removes from her jumpers but never throws away, and pieces of elastic which she uses to make her skirts and bras fit better.

Under that, we discovered the box with the letters. Unfortunately, it was tied with a ribbon and a very complex bow. We didn't think we could replicate it and were afraid we would be discovered, so we left without opening the box.

Mom's family is from the north of the country. Her mom died when she was quite young, and Mom was sent to boarding school along with her four brothers. My grandfather remarried and moved to Australia when his youngest child, my mom, went to university. I have never met him, but Ella and I speak to him twice a year at Christmas and on our birthdays. Every now and then, a package arrives from Australia, but the contents are always meant for much younger children.

Mom has four older brothers, but only one is still alive. Uncle John is an oil rig engineer, which is quite adventurous and totally impressive. He emails mom all the time and sends her amazing pictures of storms and dolphins. Uncle John is our favourite uncle, and even though we see him only once a year at Christmas, we know everything about him and his amazing life at sea. He is a very good writer, and his vivid descriptions of life on an oil rig are read again and again by the whole family. Mom's three other brothers died suddenly of cardiac arrest, two within months of each other. I have vague memories of my uncles at family gatherings, but they died when I was quite young, and I mostly know them from the pictures on Mom's dressing table. As it turns out, Hypertrophic Cardiomyopathy (HMC) runs in our family, and it is a disease that can get very dangerous for some people. Mom also has HCM, but she never appears sickly. She is simply Mom—fun and full of energy. Sometimes she feels a little dizzy, such as when she dries her hair upside down, but I don't think this has anything to do with HMC. The only time Mom got us all worried was when she got the flu a few years ago. Her lungs filled with fluid and she couldn't breathe properly. Ever since, the whole family gets flu shots every October. It is one of those things we have to live with. We know she has HMC, but it doesn't seem to make any difference in her life or ours. Hers is probably a very mild condition.

Mom left her office job when I was born and has been steadily gaining weight ever since. I don't think she liked working outside the home very much as she never talks about it and has never showed an interest in returning. She seems to be perfectly happy and content taking care of all of us, and she is a terrific cook. She cooks more than anyone can possibly eat, but I guess this is her way of showing her love.

Oddly enough, Mom has very rigid views about eating and body shape. She rarely follows any of her own advice, but she offers Ella and I regular pearls of wisdom about our weight or what we should be eating and when. Mom says that when she was 23 her waist was so small that her boyfriends could close their hands around it. I tried to get my boyfriend James to wrap his hands around my waist, but it would have taken three of his hands for that to work. I even asked Dad to try it, but the results were about the same. Mom's waist must have been absolutely tiny. You wouldn't know that looking at her now, but I have seen a picture of her when she was younger, standing in front of a three-way mirror, where she looks like a Hollywood star. I keep this picture on my wall for inspiration.

I wonder how Mom feels about her body now. It must make her a little depressed to have lost her amazing figure. She says that at her age it is impossible to lose weight, and Dad doesn't seem to mind that she is overweight.

I was only twelve when Mom took me to the Swiss Slimming Centre and asked them to make me look like a slim young lady. They weighed me and pinched me to get my BMI. I felt like a blob next to these thin, stylish women with their notepads and serious gazes. I promised myself I wouldn't disappoint them, or Mom, who spent a lot of money for me to be there.

They started me on the boiled chicken diet, which was very simple to follow, although extremely bland and boring. I was only allowed to eat boiled chicken without the skin for a whole week. I lost 7kg, which I then regained over the rest of the month.

This was the beginning of a marathon of diets. Weight Watchers, Nutrisystem, The Pineapple Diet, Juicing . . . I tried them all, and they all worked. The problem was as soon as something worked, Mom would start worrying that I was losing too much weight and she'd cook all of my absolute favourite meals. Crazy, eh? And she still does it to this day as soon as I lose any weight.

Sometimes, it's simply not worth arguing with Mom, because she knows everything! It goes like this:

Mom: Can I make you a coffee? How do you want it?
Me: I like it black, Mom, no milk or sugar.
The coffee arrives, milky and sweet, and sometimes with a beaten egg yolk in it.
Me: I can't drink this, Mom. I like my coffee black.
Mom: Nobody drinks their coffee black. You are beginning to look like an Aids victim.

How can I argue with this logic? There is really no other way to say it: Mom is a feeder and our whole family is fat—except for me, that is. My body shape is normal for my age, but it does tend to fluctuate when I let myself go.

Which I occasionally do.

Dad

Dad is a character. Around him, everything is an invention. He sits in a chair which he customized by adding shelves on either side of him. He'll have a coffee in one hand and a cigarette in the other, chain smoking and discussing politics while the TV is blaring in the background. When he is at home, whether it is winter or summer, he wears the same aging red ski jacket over greying white boxer shorts. A communist in a capitalist world, he is waiting for the revolution.

To the dismay of the rest of the family, Dad is an early riser—like, a *really* early riser. I am talking 3:30 a.m. He bangs and clangs his way out of bed and then, with a new idea in his head, he'll start noisily tinkering, completely oblivious to my seriously important teenage need for sleep. He could be sawing, hammering, or gluing something smelly. All his inventions work, but they are never pretty. There was the time he glued his glasses with a blob of epoxy, and, despite Mom's protestations, went to work wearing them.

29

Mom and Dad met during their last year of university, and it was love at first sight. They became totally inseparable, and when graduation came, after going home for the summer, Mom followed Dad to our town and got a job locally. Following her own advice, she didn't move in with him. Instead she shared a flat with two other girls. Dad couldn't bear not being near her all the time, so he proposed within months, and Mom, after making him wait a full day and a half, accepted.

Mom has her own box of letters, one for every day they were apart during that summer after university. Unlike Mamgu Winny, who is keeping her secrets, Mom has let me read a couple of her letters. They are super romantic. Looking at my dad now, I can't imagine him writing those letters. There is one in particular that is totally *tortured soul* writing, which my dad absolutely is not. He said, amongst other things, "You don't know what it's like to be the middle child," and that she, my Mom, was the only woman who truly understood him and brought out the best in him. I hope someday I meet a man who writes me letters like that and tells me I am the only woman who gets him. I don't think my current boyfriend James is that type. The most romantic thing he's ever said to me was that my eyes are a beautiful colour. I am grateful for that, but how unimaginative is he compared to my dad?

Dad is very outdoorsy. Mom calls him her *boy scout* even though he's never really been one. When we go camping, he can pitch our large family tent in under twenty minutes on his own. Ella and I hand him the pegs and the tools while Mom unpacks the car and airs out our sleeping bags. Mom and Dad are so coordinated they don't even need to exchange

30

a word. Within thirty minutes, they are finished and enjoying a glass of wine while we tear through the crisps and Oreos.

Mom and Dad are big fans of festivals. We go to a minimum of two music festivals a year, and there I see a side of my parents which I don't see at home. It's probably what they were like before they had kids, real jobs, and obligations.

Ella and I have been going to festivals since we were babies. We usually go with three other families and pitch our tents in a circle with a gazebo in the middle. There are costumes, wigs, magic tricks, dancing, and on one occasion there was even drugs! Yes, I said it—*drugs*. Last year, at the Big Chill festival, Mom took drugs. To be fair, she didn't know that one of their friends had slipped something into the drinks, but nevertheless, it happened. I've never seen Mom the way she was that day, and I hope I never see that again. She was in a state all night. Laughing, singing, calling out to strangers and dancing wildly around our tent. Dad was not ruffled and found the whole thing hilarious. I could see how amused he was, even though he tried hard to keep a straight face as Mom danced around his chair and screeched like a banshee. Finally, as the sun came up, Mom ran out of steam and fell asleep face down on her mat. When she woke up, she claimed that the whole experience was horrible, and we should all stay well clear of drugs. But I could tell she'd had fun.

Dad is quite shy around strangers and it takes a bit of time for him to warm up to people. I can tell when he is feeling uncomfortable because he leans against the wall and looks at his phone until Mom comes over and draws him into the conversation. If she is not around to help, he soon seeks out

Ella or me and we'll go for a walk together or on some other kind of expedition. I love those times with my dad because he never criticizes how I look or what I do. Instead, he listens intently to my stories and asks loads of questions, always encouraging me and making me feel interesting and the centre of his world. This is a wonderful quality in my father, and I try to imitate him when I'm with my friends.

Dad works at a phone company, managing a team of architects. He says he doesn't need any architects, but his boss keeps hiring them as a favour to his political buddies. I'm not sure what he does at work all day, but when he gets home in the late afternoon and after a big meal, he retires to the bedroom with the shutters firmly shut and sleeps for a couple of hours. He calls this time *holy*, and nobody is allowed to make a sound.

Dad is not one for waste. He sees gold in every dustbin and finds potential in the junk our neighbours discard. When he passes by a pile of garbage he always stops to look. Usually, he'll find something to load onto the roof rack and bring home. There are no less than four washing machines and two fridges in our basement awaiting repair. The one washing machine he did repair doesn't really wash or rinse properly, but Mom puts up with it.

There is real love in our family.

Chapter Seven

Whiteheath School for Girls

As a middle-class six-year-old girl growing up in our town, there was only one school to which my parents aspired to send me—Whiteheath School for Girls. It's the Holy Grail of female education, and, of course, that was where my mother managed to secure spots for her little treasures.

Whiteheath, ruled by iron-fisted women, annually churns out 175 prim, proper, and adequately educated girls, commonly referred to in the right social circles as *Whiteheath girls*. Every boy wants a *Whiteheath girl*, if not in his kitchen, then most certainly in his bed. The school tries to thwart horny young men by stationing two armed guards on either side of the long road connecting the two gates of the sprawling estate. A tall fence topped up with broken glass discourages even the boldest of white knights.

The Whiteheath complex is dominated by a majestic main building rising over a large oval arena. School coaches come in from the bottom gate, drive up into the arena clockwise, unload the screeching young ladies at the top of the hour and drive out the top gate. Once 2,000 of us are unloaded, assembly begins. The two headmistresses point to one unfortunate pupil, who then has to walk up the steps to the podium overlooking the arena and mumble morning prayers to the 4,000 eyes staring at her. With this ritual completed, we file into our classrooms, and the giant arena remains deserted until the final bell that signals the end of the school day.

Silently waiting at the right of the arena is the pillar of our spiritual education—a Roman Catholic Church, complete with cupola, priest, and aging cantor. The church holds about sixty of us, standing once a week for a two-hour mass. Oh how we loathe our turn at mass, gagging on the sickly smell of sweat mixed with burning incense as the priest, who also provides our religious education, leads the service. Father Andrew, in his long black robes, likes to block the doorway to the classroom so his lecherous, wandering holy hands always stand between me and our twenty-minute break.

Whiteheath school is quite strict and perhaps a bit old-fashioned. To go anywhere as a class, even at our age, we have to form a line of twos based on height. At 1.74m, I am quite tall, so I always end up at the back next to my friend Lila. We march like this to the school's church, at national holiday parades, and on cultural day trips. Whiteheath requires two types of school uniform in addition to the sports kit. One is for regular school days and the other for special events and every time we leave the school. This second uniform is quite expensive and can only be bought at one department store in town. It's used four or five times a year at most, and parents complain about the cost all the time. But the school will not budge. As a result, many of the girls end up with uniforms they've had since Year Seven. The result is a far cry from the formal look for which Whiteheath is aiming, and the headmistress has often banned the worst cases of misfit uniforms from the big national parade.

When I started secondary school, my mom bought me a uniform which was several sizes too big on purpose. It completely dwarfed me. Two years later, the sleeves were up to my elbows, the skirt had been let out all the way, and even then it was too short. Mom was forced to purchase a new one, and she was not at all pleased about it. Finances are always a bit tight at home, especially with private school fees and only Dad working.

Our school day is long—from 8:30 in the morning until 4:00 in the afternoon. Two evenings a week I stay after school for study groups, so I don't get home until 7 p.m. We get two ten-minute breaks and a one-hour break for lunch.

I love breaks. Most of the girls run to join the queue at the canteen, but not me. I make a beeline for the toilets to meet up with my friends for a quick fag, to take the edge off the midday hunger without adding any calories. A thin cloud of smoke rises above the toilet block during every break, but I've never seen a teacher come to investigate. We all know smoking is really bad for you, but being fat is much, much worse.

I've always found school to be quite easy and I'm getting decent grades with just a little bit of work. I always do my homework on the coach, and usually I also have time to finish my makeup. We are not really allowed makeup at school, but none of us would ever be seen barefaced. We just avoid the obvious giveaways such as eyeshadow and lipstick and tone down everything else.

As much as our headmistress dislikes girls with makeup, she *really* hates short skirts. Sometimes she walks around during break with a measuring tape and rounds up the worst offenders, who are then forced to wear one of her loaner *nun skirts*. I convinced Mom to shorten my skirt enough to look fashionable, but not so short as to run the risk of being hauled into the headmistress's office.

Ginny has a different strategy. She is never seen standing by anyone who cares about the length of her skirt. Her skirts are so short that you can actually see her underwear if she bends over even just a little bit. Even when I tell her I can see the colour of her panties, she totally doesn't care. Her mom thinks the fashion police are ridiculous and should be abolished, so she lets Ginny wear anything she wants. On the rare occasions when Ginny gets caught, her mom laughs it off and buys her a new skirt. My mom, on the other hand, would not have been as generous. If I had lost the rights to one of the two £47 skirts she has to buy every year, she would probably make me pay her back out of my own pocket money. When I lost my school jumper, I hid it from her through the whole of winter. I told her I was too hot, even though I shivered at the bus stop every day. On the coldest days, and on the days the school coach was late, I would hug Ella tightly to keep warm. She pretended not to like it, but she never pushed me off. I know secretly she enjoyed the closeness and the attention.

I think my school is a little bit behind the times when it comes to rules. We have too many rules, and plenty of teachers who make sure we follow every single one. No chewing gum, no makeup, no slip-on shoes, hair tied back, tights without holes, etc., etc., etc. In my school, you are

36

more likely to get sent home for wearing a thin chain around your neck than for smoking in the bathrooms. It is a mystery to me why no teacher approaches the bathrooms during breaks, but it suits Ginny and me just fine. As soon as the bell rings, we flush the butts down the toilet, swallow a few Tic Tac's and chew spearmint gum all the way to class, where I stick my glob of gum under the desk. Ginny sticks it behind her ear, but I think that's gross.

I take the coach to school every day. That is, I take it on the days I manage to catch it. On many occasions it is quite elusive, and Mom doesn't help matters by leaving me snoozing during those mornings when she feels I've not got enough sleep the night before. On those mornings, she wakes me up late enough for me to miss the coach but too early to make a real difference in my sleep deficit. Then, in a frantic routine, Mom bundles me up into the car half-dressed and starts chasing after the coach. Once it's in sight, she'll flash her lights and beep her horn to get the driver's attention. It is a game they play, the two of them, and it is always the same. She makes all the noise and he ignores it, never stopping until he reaches his next scheduled stop in front of St. Margaret's Church. This operation causes me endless embarrassment, and I hate walking down the coach aisle while the other girls laugh and comment. I've even tried to set my own alarm, but Mom just comes into my room at night and turns it off. I love my mom more than anything, but at times she can be infuriating.

At the beginning of this year, Mom signed me up for maths tutoring. I am mostly okay with maths, but Mom, having struggled with maths herself, wants to make sure I don't fall behind. The exams at the of the year will decide which uni I go to. I want to do really well on them, so I agreed to the extra hours of tutoring. There is an evening school in the centre of town, and the best bit about it is there are boys! The school promises we will all get amazing grades in maths by following their system, and I believe it.

I find homework a lot easier since I started attending.

Chapter Eight

James

James Floyd is my current boyfriend. Most girls at my school don't have a boyfriend. Where would we meet one, after all? I am lucky, because we share a bus stop with the boys from Soames College, and I have known them since Reception. They always invite me to their parties, and I bring Ginny along for girl support. Many of the popular girls have met lots of guys through Instagram, but not me. I would be far too shy to start a discussion with a stranger online and much too afraid to go meet them in person.

I was introduced to James at a party and we hit it off right away. We like the same music, and he is really good-looking. He tells me I am beautiful and sends me a hundred text messages every day. I only send him one or two.

The best thing about James is that he has a car and his learner's permit. His parents let him drive short distances on his own, and he's agreed to teach me how to drive as well. We usually meet at the café next to the evening school where I do maths tutoring. When I finish class, he is waiting for me, the engine running. I take the driver's seat and we drive around the block several times before he takes me home. I haven't had a chance to change all the gears yet, but I know everything else. I am a careful driver and absolutely love the freedom of being able to take myself where I want, when I want. I plan to apply for my own learner's permit soon and I've been badgering Dad to get me driving lessons for my eighteenth birthday. He remains non-committal, but I think he will do it. At least, I hope he will.

Mom is very interested in James. She wants to know everything about him.

"Where does he go to school? What do his parents do? What subjects is he taking?" I showed her a picture of him on Instagram and she sent him a follow request. I told him about it, and he accepted.

Awkward! I am not sure what is worse—that she asked, or that he accepted?

Despite her meddling nature, I have to give her some credit. Mom knows a lot about boys, love, and relationships. Among other things, she says that to get boys interested I should not appear to be too available, and I think she is right. Mom knows all the tricks in the book. She has been drilling Ella and me since we were little, explaining how boys (even the older ones) are not as mysterious or clever as girls make them out to be. She suggested some very good rules to follow if I wanted to get a boy interested in me. Mom started coaching me as soon as I had my first boyfriend. She told me men are hunters and girls should play hard to get. This means not messaging them unless they message first, being slightly unavailable, and never, ever whining and winging.

This last one is never a problem for me. I am the sort of girl who is generally easy-going and willing to go along with most plans. Ella and Dad can argue for hours about what to watch on TV. They flick through the options, watch several trailers, look at Rotten Tomatoes scores, and by the time they finally decide on a movie, it's either too late to watch it or it's a really poor compromise. Mom doesn't care what we watch and spends most of the evening catching up on her chores, loading the dishwasher, making popcorn, and folding the laundry. When a decision on what to watch is finally made, she will glance at the television sporadically while doing other things, unless the movie is a thriller or action adventure.

I prefer reality shows, especially ones about health and beauty, but nobody else in my house wants to watch those, so I often sit on the sofa with my headphones on, eating my popcorn, and watching my own shows on my laptop. Mamgu Winny likes love stories and has become addicted to soap operas from Turkey, of all places. Sometimes she dozes on the sofa, but often she watches her soaps in her own flat, lying on her bed. Dad checks on her at the end of the evening, and turns off her TV and bedside lamp. I love evenings with the family. There is laughter, jokes, popcorn, and chocolate. All of the days stress simply disappears. I am a lucky girl, and I know it.

James and I have been together for over two months. Until recently, there had only been lots of kissing (with tongues), but recently I have given him free rein above the waist. I don't really like all his heavy breathing and I hate all the fumbling with my breasts, but it is a small price to pay to have a steady boyfriend. He is my fourth boyfriend since Year Six, and definitely the best one so far. He says he likes skinny girls, *borderline anorexic*. This must mean that I look thin through his eyes, even though I can't really see it when I look in the mirror.

The other three boyfriends I've had were only for a week each, and only one kissed me. I'm not sure they really count, but it makes me sound more experienced than all the other girls in my friend group. There are girls at my school who say they've had sex and countless boyfriends, but in our friend group we are all virgins and totally clueless when it comes to boys. Mom reminds me that we should not think of boys as mature, and that they are often shy and a bit afraid of girls. Looking at them throwing spit-balls at each other during tutoring classes, I can't help but agree with her.

I cannot say I'm particularly mature with guys either. I have real trouble giving people bad news, so I never leave my boyfriends. In fact, when I break up with someone, I make sure they never find out. It becomes a closely-guarded secret which only reveals itself over time and through careful observation. I stop answering my phone. I am busy when the boy in question asks me out. And when we're together, I don't let him kiss me.

You get the picture. Hopefully, so does the soon-to-be-ex-boyfriend. You see, I am a proper coward when it comes to disappointing people, and I see myself as a decent sort of human being, which means I cannot break up with a guy via text message. My method may be slow and laborious, and might even be described as torturous, but it works. Everybody eventually gets the picture and may even be so fed up with me that they're actually relieved to be the one to leave me. Of course, should they leave me first, there's always the risk that I will fall in love with them anew. Breaking up with a boy is a dangerous minefield for me.

42

Boyfriends are a hot topic at our all-girls school. In the toilets I've heard a lot of bragging stories, but I take them with a grain of salt. One girl even described in detail the technique for a blowjob. She says she does them often, but I don't really believe her. I think she read about it somewhere and she's just making the whole thing up. I can't imagine me ever doing that. It sounds super gross. I retch just thinking about it.

Though, there is one thing I want to do before university, and that is to have sex. I don't want to be the only virgin in the year, and every day a new girl brags of having left the vestal virgin ranks. Mom says I shouldn't worry, but it is easy for her to say. She lost her virginity at fifteen with a random guy on vacation. Looking at her now, it's hard to imagine she had a wild side to her. She is so… *mumsy*, and I'm happy about that. Unlike other mums, she's very open about sex. All she wants me to do is make sure I'm safe and use a condom, and I totally agree.

I learned all I know about sex from Mamgu Winny's encyclopedia for women. It's a nine-volume encyclopedia which contains everything a woman should know, from cake making to changing nappies. It's totally old-fashioned, but I still love it. It occupies an entire shelf of our main bookcase.

There is a long stain across several volumes from when one of Mamgu Winny's cats peed on it.

Chapter Nine

Ella

My sister Ella is two years younger than I am and 20cm shorter. She was born a month and a half early, and Mom is very protective of her because of that. Ella loves to eat, and Mom loves to feed her. Well, Mom loves to feed everyone, but Ella in particular because she was born underweight. The poor kid never stood a chance at being thin. Mom never took *her* to the Swiss Slimming Centre, probably believing it would be a waste of time and money.

Ella never claimed to like school, and her grades are terrible. Every time she has an exam coming up, she develops some sort of illness, including once getting appendicitis before her geography exam. Last year, she wrote in her history exam that Hitler committed suicide because he couldn't conquer Greece. I mean, really?

The headmistress of Whiteheath rightly decided that Ella would not be able to cope with the requirements of the school, so to her great relief, she went to the local comprehensive with all the other neighbourhood kids.

Once Ella started secondary school, she jumped on the diet bandwagon on her own, but with mixed results. Despite her early successes, she never managed to control her weight for very long. She is always happier when she is thin and is often in a foul mood when her weight gets the upper hand, but luckily, her bad moods don't come often and only last a few hours.

Ella has a face which cannot hide her feelings. Her booming voice gave her the nickname *The Siren*, and I think she is secretly proud of it. Everything Ella does is big. She storms through the kitchen door, drops her school bag where she stands and starts recounting a story she overheard on the school bus. Her facts are almost always wrong, but they are substantial and imaginative, and she supports her version of the story passionately. She waves her hands furiously until she runs out of steam and then plops her ample frame upon the nearest chair, puffing and huffing.

Ella is adored by her many friends, who love to confide in her because she always has something nice to say. She has smiling eyes, big movements, and almost always misinterprets what she hears. She makes up stories and then is the first to believe them. I'm furious when she recreates the past in her own utterly false way, but I can't stay angry for long. I absolutely adore my sister and her quirky ways.

Embarrassed to ask for the smallest of favours, Ella explodes occasionally in public in the most spectacular and foul-mouthed fashion. When it comes to my sister, babies and animals are always cute, the government is always crooked, Mom is always right, I am always wrong, and friends are loyal and loving until she feels betrayed over the most trivial of slights. My sister is very hard and very soft at

46

the same time and carries a strong sense of responsibility. Her room is constantly a mess and her side of our shared bathroom is a perpetual reason for arguments between us. Despite her big personality, she also has a weird sort of shyness and pride. She is too shy to ask for the smallest of favours and yet she will explode spectacularly in public when her pride gets hurt.

I have not always been good to my sister. Sometimes I feel guilty when I see her face crumple because of something stupid I've said without thinking. She is sensitive about a lot of things, and of course, being close to my sister, I know them all. It's super easy to push her buttons, and sometimes when she exasperates me, I do. We are ten sizes apart, yet she'll sneak into my room and borrow my clothes, my makeup, and my jewellery without asking. When I can't find a favourite jumper or belt after looking everywhere she'll just sit there and say nothing. I have to look her straight in the eye and accuse her of having my stuff. Tail between her legs, she'll go and retrieve the missing item. I suppose this back-and-forth is fairly common between sisters, but it still makes me really mad when it happens.

Ella is good with her money, much better than I am. She receives pocket money, just as I do, but she also works every Saturday at Mamgu Winny's shop, helping customers and learning the business. She enjoys those Saturdays, and Mamgu Winny has had discussions with Dad about letting Ella have the shop after she retires and Ella graduates. This would suit everyone greatly, as nobody else, including our cousins, is even remotely interested in taking it over. Dad would have preferred to shut the whole thing down and for Ella to do something else, but Ella insists she wants to have her own business and that she'll make it work. Dad will have to compensate his brother, but the business has declined over the years so it would not amount to much. Ella has many good ideas on revamping the shop, but none of them will happen while it's under Mamgu Winny's iron rule. If it were me, I would have rebelled and probably left already, but Ella is biding her time and making herself as useful as possible, learning as much as she can while she waits.

My sister loves hats. She has an extensive collection for summer and winter. She also has three different bikes. She bought two of them with her own pocket money, and the other was a Christmas present. She likes to ride her bike everywhere. Often, she'll carry one of her friends in the front. I think it looks like a circus trick when they do that, but she assures me it's not hard at all. Right! She can even climb Hillside Row without getting off her bike. Instead, she'll stand up on the pedals, and to everyone's amazement manages to stay on all the way to our front door.

We sisters are as different as can be, but there is real love between us.

Chapter Ten

Cats, Dogs, Hamsters and Other Animals

Mom loves all kinds of animals. When she was a little girl she used to roam her neighbourhood looking for abandoned kittens, which she would then carry home and feed with an eyedropper. Once she was in boarding school she was not allowed to have any pets, so she started feeding a mouse in the storage room of the school. When she was found out, she almost got expelled, as the mouse turned out to be a whole family of mice, and they had eaten through the entire supply of school pillowcases and breakfast cereal.

I grew up with pets. First, we had cats. Lots of cats. Both indoor and outdoor cats. Every chair in our house had a sleeping cat on it, and very often we had new kittens. Once, even one of our male cats had kittens. Yes, I know it's impossible, but somehow it happened. Mom and Dad kept having heated discussions about neutering our cats, but Mom had her own ideas on the matter and there was no changing her mind. Nothing would convince her to deprive any living being of the joys of sex and motherhood, so our feline population multiplied.

I had my own cat called Fundula, who lived in my room and slept in my bed. She was a beautiful cat with very long hair, in three different colours. One night she had kittens—right in my bed. Mom woke me up and cleaned up the mess, but I was delighted. All of our other cats would hide when they had kittens, but Fundula trusted me enough to have her kittens in my bed. I was enchanted and told everyone who would listen about the wonderful bond I shared with my cat.

When I was eight, I suddenly developed an allergy to cats. It started mildly enough, with itchy eyes and a bit of sneezing, but soon I started wheezing. When I got a full-blown asthma attack, we all knew the cats had to go. Within the family there were many theories as to why my allergies had suddenly popped up and what caused them, but Mom was convinced that at the root of it was my relationship with my cat. When Fundula had her kittens, she changed from a loving pet to a mutant tiger. She would attack me and scratch me unexpectedly and without provocation. I ended up being very afraid of her and avoided her at all costs. Our GP told Mom that allergies don't develop that way, but Mom, who is a doctor in disguise, knew better. In fact, to this day, when I get wheezy, Mom never takes me seriously and says it's psychological. It drives me crazy!

Whether my allergies are psychological or not remains open to debate, but what was undisputed was that the cats had to find other homes. There were so many cats and so few takers that in desperation Mom put all the cats in the car and drove them out into the country, where she paid a kind lady to take care of them. At least two of them showed up at our door several years later, but Mom remained unmoved and drove them back to their foster home.

With the cats gone, there was a gaping hole in our lives, and there were heated debates as to what kind of pet we should get next. Mom, being Mom, did the unexpected and came back one day with a baby goat in the car. The goat ended up in our bathtub looking miserable and disoriented while we tried to make her comfortable with our duvets and pillows. When Dad got home that evening, he put the goat in the car and we never saw it again.

While this was going on, Ella had been secretly saving her money, and one Saturday came home carrying a little cage. In it was a very smelly animal which she immediately took to her bedroom. It turned out she had been sold a ferret, and over her screaming protestations Mom took the smelly furry thing back to the pet shop.

At that point, Dad sensibly interjected and suggested we get a dog—a hypoallergenic one. This is how Gourounelious came into our lives. Gourounelious was an apricot miniature poodle with a huge appetite for love and food. I came up with the name by combining Greek and Latin in one elegant made up word which means, I suppose, a small pig with Roman origins. Gourounelious turned out to be a handful. He demanded endless attention and he couldn't be left alone, not even for a minute, or he would bring the house down. No amount of training could get him to stop his mischief, so after six months of him crying and the neighbourhood complaining, Mom gave him away. The story has a happy ending, as he ended up with an old lady who was always at home and was quite lonely. Gourounelious got her out of the house, and when they were not out walking he would contentedly snooze in her lap.

Over the next two years, we had several pet experiments. Mom brought home ducks, chicks, and rabbits. The chicks ended up being roosters who, blinded by the city lights, would wake up the neighbours at all times of the night. The rabbits escaped their hutch and ate the neighbour's prized flowerbed. As for the ducks, their habitat proved a challenge. I dug up part of the garden and lined it with bin bags to make a pond for them to swim in, which very soon became a disgusting, smelly pit of standing water and rotting duck food. Dad filled it back in with dirt one afternoon, talking about health and safety. The next day the ducks disappeared.

Our final pets, the ones which stayed with us the longest, were John and Trixie, named after Uncle John and a cartoon character from one of Ella's comic books. John was a pink hamster and Trixie a chestnut one. They soon fell in love and we had babies again. Hamsters store things in their cheeks, especially when they get startled. Something must have startled John, because he decided to transport his babies in his cheeks, and they all died.

Six months later, we had more babies, and John got his own cage. These babies survived into adulthood, but not without first being sucked up by the vacuum cleaner and then rescued in what was an extremely messy but successful operation. Trixie continued having babies, and soon we had too many. Mom decided to throw us a big party for the sole purpose of handing out the extra hamsters in goodie bags. My friends were delighted with the novelty and happily accepted their new pets. Not so much their moms. The next day, one by one, the hamsters were returned by outraged mothers who'd discovered that they had unwittingly become the owners of a rodent. Mom had to accept defeat and she returned Trixie and all of her offspring to the pet shop.

We kept John. He was the perfect pet for our family.

Chapter Eleven

The Best Friend Group Ever

My friend group is amazing. The inner circle is five of us, and we totally support each other in every way. Ginny, Hannah, Megan, Lila, and me. We have all pledged that we'll stay close after the end of this year, even though it looks as if we will be taking very different paths.

Ginny is my closest friend. She is the cool one, because her mom lets her get away with the most. Ginny has the most freedom, the most generous allowance, and a larger selection of trendy clothes than the rest of us put together. She's always happy to share, and we all do. Our sizes vary a bit, but we manage to squeeze into each other's clothes.

None of us are serious smokers. In fact, I think Hannah has never inhaled (ha ha), but we all make for the bathrooms as soon as the school bell rings. As unlikely a place as it may be, it's in the Whiteheath bathrooms where all of our life plans take shape. Ginny always has a cigarette and Lila often pinches a menthol one from her mom. The rest of us share drags off the others, and through the cloud of nicotine we discuss boys, makeup, clothes, and diets.

We tell each other everything. Hannah is the one who's always in the middle of some kind of drama. None of it seems that stressful to me, but to Hannah, who is a drama major, everything is drama. The small catastrophes of her life, discussed in great detail, is a staple of our daily smoking breaks. She takes all of our advice gratefully and follows none of it. Hannah is one of two, but her twin could not be any more different. Hannah is short and chubby, with what used to be brown hair which is now blonde with some pink peeking through. Jessica, who is Hannah's twin, is my height, with her hair severely pulled back and her nose always deep in some kind of esoteric book. Whiteheath has a policy of separating twins into different forms, so we don't see Jessica very often. Ginny is in the same form as Jessica, but she may as well be part of our form. She's always hanging out with us and is my very best friend.

Megan came to Whiteheath from Australia with her mom and older brother. Her parents are divorced, and her dad stayed behind with his new family. Megan never speaks about her dad, nor her life in Australia. She lives with her family at her grandparent's house, which is our friend group's headquarters. It's right across the street from the school and has a basement where we often go to hang out together after school. Megan's grandmother used to teach English at Whiteheath, which is how Megan managed to secure a spot midterm in Year Seven. Megan is tiny and very, very thin. She is lovely, with long, flowing hair and a nose dotted with freckles. She has the best grades out of everyone in our group, but she is also the most anxious about school. I think it's because her mom always insists that she has to become financially independent when she grows up and not expect any man to support her. I am lucky, because Megan is in all my classes and we sit next to each other. We're also in the same study group and compare notes to make sure we haven't missed anything. There is a little bit of academic rivalry between us, but it benefits us both as we try to outdo each other.

Lila is the artist. She is extremely creative. She makes her own clothes, paints murals on her garage door, bakes elaborate cakes, and has her own recipes for face masks and creams. Her presents are always something she's made, and even the cards and the packaging are unusual and worth keeping. I have a whole drawer of Lila's creations. I'm sure someday they'll be worth something. Lila wants to be a designer, preferably to the stars. She is hardworking, single-minded and stubborn. If anyone could reach her dreams, it would be her.

She spent all last summer working for free at Signature Creations, the most prestigious wedding dress shop in town. She mostly served customers and brought drinks and coffee to the bridal groups, but sometimes she was allowed to sit in during sampling sessions with designers and manufacturers. She took loads of notes and showed us an entire notebook filled with ideas on how to improve the designs of the dresses. Signature Creations has already offered her a fulltime job once we graduate, but Lila has much bigger plans. The minute we are out of school, she plans to move to Paris, the haute couture capital of Europe, and study at one of the many design schools while working part-time. She's been saving for this trip for the past few years and she's really good with money. I admire her courage and determination.

My own pocket money disappears as soon as it hits my bank account. To be fair, it's not a lot of money to begin with, but Mom always slips me a bit extra when I go out. She says she never wants me to be without taxi money or feel as if I have to get into someone's car because I can't afford the fare home. To be honest, this taxi money always ends up being cigarette money. Mom is no dummy. Every time I am about to walk out the door, she demands to see the twenty she has given me for taxi money, and when I don't have it, she'll reach into her bag and give me a new one, threatening all the time that she will dock my pocket money. But of course, she never does.

The hottest topic in our friendship group is diets and fashion. I am always on a diet and so is Ginny. Hannah tries, or at least she says she does, but she must be eating secretly, because her weight has been going only one direction—*up*. Every now and then she comes to school waving around information on some new diet she is going to try, but then we never hear about it again and she remains as chubby as ever.

Ginny is the expert on weight control. She is the one who comes up with the best diets. Together, we tried the *Rainbow Diet*. This is a pretty interesting diet, as fads go. You eat one colour of food per day, except for every Wednesday, when you fast completely. So, for example, Mondays is the colour red. You eat half a cup of strawberries for breakfast, half a red pepper for lunch, and then another half-cup of strawberries for dinner. Ginny managed to make it the whole week, but I only lasted until Wednesday night, when I went to the kitchen and demolished an entire frozen pizza, eight fish fingers, and a loaf of bread.

The *Five Bites* diet tasted better, but it was super hard to put into practice. You can eat basically anything you want, but you only get five bites for each meal. It goes like this: Five bites of oatmeal for breakfast, five bites of a sandwich for lunch, and five bites of pasta for dinner. I personally prefer to eat nothing than to push my plate away after five bites, or worse yet, throw out my sandwich when I'm really hungry. Ginny says this one works only if you have great strength of character, so I suppose I'm a complete wimp! This one was a total flop for me.

Mom told me that all these diets are ridiculous, and the best way to lose weight is to eat sensibly, but I have seen her eat an entire box of macaroons in one sitting, and that is obviously not sensible. I'm not even sure *sensible* works for me. It's all or nothing. I prefer to fast all day and eat all my calories at dinner than to have a salad for lunch or a chicken breast for dinner. It simply doesn't work for me this way.

Megan and Lila, on the other hand, are the sensible-eating types. I'll watch them picking at their lunches at school or leaving without finishing a plate of fries. That whole concept is completely alien to me. When they sit there chatting in front of a half-full bowl of chicken nuggets, I use all of my willpower not to finish their lunches as well as mine. I think it's unfair that life is so easy for them. I wish I could just stop eating when I'm full and be able to ignore the food in front of me when it has been paid for. This is actually quite weird, when I really stop to think about it. Probably it has something to do with Mamgu Winny insisting that our strength came from the last bite of food on our plates, so we have to eat it. Of course, I know all of this is nonsense, but the habit is so ingrained within my psyche that I hear this little voice whispering, "Finish it. Finish it."

And then, I do!

SUMMER

Chapter Twelve

Ginny

School is out! Exams are done and dusted, and I did great. The sun is shining, and I have a whole summer to relax before the final year of school. It will be a killer year in terms of exams and selecting a university, but it will also be the beginning of my adult life. But you know what? I'm not going to think about any of that now. Not when I have two lazy months stretched out in front of me. I have few plans and lots of bikinis. Hurrah for summer!

Time to take stock of the most important thing in regard to summer—my weight. No one can see me in a bikini until I lose the kilos I gained during exams. I'm a bit embarrassed by how much I let myself go in the last month, but Mom was always coming around with snacks. The study time was hard, and I was always hungry. I have not dared to step on a scale, but I am sure I gained at least five kilos—five ugly, fatty, disgusting kilos which make me look like a Teletubby. I'm thinking with the *Nescafe Diet* I can lose it all in two weeks, enough time for me to look okay before Julie's pool party. I don't know Julie well, but she is close to my best friend Ginny, so I am going as her plus-one. Ginny is in my year but in a different form. At school, we are inseparable. We are Ginny and Winny, or as everyone calls us, *The Winny Ginnies*. Unlike my other friends, she is very confident and outgoing. She always wears lots of makeup and looks quite a bit older than the rest of us. The boys we know all lust after her, and a few claim to have slept with her. Ginny neither confirms nor denies the rumours, which makes her even more popular and mysterious. She is, of course, very skinny, with an amazing body. I am not sure how she does it, because she is always munching on something unhealthy.

Ginny is my idol. One day I will be as skinny and as confident as she is. We both know she calls the shots in our friendship, but I don't really mind. She is full of exciting ideas and we are always doing something fun together. Ginny has an older half-sister who is already engaged, and two other half-brothers she never sees. Her entire family is really unusual, what Mom calls *bohemians*. I personally think they are glamorous. I wish my mom was a little bit like Ginny's. Mrs. Pollard is always dressed to the nines, even when there is nowhere to go. She glides around the house in impossibly high heels, dressed entirely in black, with her silky long blonde hair swirling around her. She always dangles an unlit cigarette in the corner of her mouth and carries a glass of something fizzy in one hand. I have never seen her light her cigarette, but Ginny says her mom secretly smokes in the garden, even though she pretends to have quit. Mrs. Pollard is on husband number three—Ginny's dad— who is rarely there. When I visit, Mrs. Pollard orders takeaway for us, but she never eats anything herself. She usually pours a large glass of wine and sits at the end of the table listening to our stories while we eat. Sometimes she asks questions, but I am sure she doesn't hear our answers, because she can never remember who is who in our friendship group, or even what subjects Ginny is taking at school.

Julie, who is having the party, is one of the popular girls at school. She lives in a giant house with a huge outdoor pool. Her parents agreed to let her have a party to celebrate the end of term and doing well on her exams. Everyone who is anybody at school will be there, and I can't wait. My boyfriend James was not invited, but I am relieved about that. I want to enjoy myself and dance instead of putting up with his wandering hands in some dark corner.

Let the countdown begin!

Chapter Thirteen

Rosie

Rosie is my best friend in the world, even closer than Ginny. We grew up together at Hillside Row and she is almost like a sister to me. We are always at each other's houses and our moms are close friends. There is only one month between our birthdays and we grew up sharing everything—clothes, toys, books, and even my subscription to Spotify.

Now I am a full 15cm taller than she is, but we can still share most things, because we are the same size. Rosie has a very pretty face, but she really loves to eat, and she never denies herself anything. She pretends to diet every now and then, but we both know she is not serious, and her efforts never last more than a day or two.

Rosie and I share a common diary. It is something we started in Year Four, and we have finished several volumes over the years. Our diary travels between our homes and we write our deepest thoughts to each other. Sometimes we just write about silly things or complain about boys and about our siblings. When we're old, we plan on moving in together in a house by the sea, where we will spend our days taking care of our grandchildren, reading our diaries and remembering being young.

Rosie is not very stylish, and she doesn't have any interest in makeup and clothes. Even though we are almost seventeen, she has never had a boyfriend, and she doesn't want one either. She says she is perfectly happy sitting on my bed eating Doritos and talking about music. At her sweet-sixteen birthday party, she only invited three girls from her school. We all sat together in the living room drinking fruit punch and playing musical chairs.

If only she would let herself experience some of the parties at my school, where everybody is drinking, smoking, and making out without any adult in sight. Also, although I have not seen this myself, Ginny says she has seen some of the kids smoking weed as well. Rosie is so innocent sometimes.

Rosie and I share a secret obsession with The Vamps. There are four singers in the group, so we each like two of them. I have the lead singer Brad and the drummer Tristan, and she likes James, the lead guitarist, and Connor, who plays base. We send them emails and write about them in our diary. I find Brad extremely sexy, but I would also date Tristan if he asked me.

Of course, I don't talk about The Vamps with anyone else other than Rosie. They are not very popular with the other girls at our school, and Ginny even made a face once when I mentioned adding one of their songs to our common playlist. So instead, I listen to them during my runs, in the shower and in the privacy of Rosie's bedroom. *Somebody to You* is my favourite song. I have a playlist with only that song on endless repeat. I can listen to it twelve times during a 5K run.

We even saw them perform live once. Rosie used her bulk to get us all the way to the front and it was amazing. The field was muddy and there must have been a million screaming girls present. We had a brilliant time and even got to take pictures where our idols can be seen very clearly right behind us. We took pictures of each other, but it was a bit like a selfie. Rosie still keeps hers as her lock screen.

I changed mine to a group picture of our friend group.

Chapter Fourteen

The Nescafe Diet

This is the simplest and most effective diet for quick results. You eat and drink nothing except Nescafe. I suppose I could also drink tea, if only I liked tea, which I don't. This diet is my own invention and it suits my personality, which is, as I mentioned before, *all or nothing*. The truth is, Mom has banned this diet and I am not technically allowed to go without food for days on end, but it's not as if I'm going to announce it to anyone except Ginny, who totally gets why I diet and won't give me away.

Mom is normally quite eagle-eyed when it comes to what Ella and I eat, but recently she has been quite preoccupied and absent-minded. I don't really like to think about it, but she and Dad have been having some heated arguments when they think we aren't listening, and I can't help but think this has something to do with it. My room is right over their bedroom, and even though I can only hear every second or third word, I have been listening to their muffled arguments. I'm not quite sure what the problem is, but it must be serious, because they argue every single night. Something about Dad being depressed and unhappy and looking for his path to happiness, but he says he doesn't know why or where that path may be. Mom argues back about him travelling all the time and not paying attention to us anymore. Accuses him of having a midlife crisis and tells him to get over it. My parents have been together for a very long time, and until recently, I had never once heard them argue. They usually agree on everything, which is a bit of a pain if you're a teenager, but also really nice when we go out as a family. I hope they stay together forever!

Anyway, back to the Nescafe Diet. My plan is to always be out of the house at lunch, visiting friends or at the mall or something. I can come home just after dinnertime and say I ate at a friend's house. I never eat breakfast anyway, and it's only for a week to ten days. If I keep busy and out of the house, I won't even be hungry. That's the real secret here— keep busy and go shopping for clothes. Ginny and I have found all the shops with the good bargains and we can easily stay at the mall all day, riffling through all the summer sales. That's my other plan. I will buy everything one size smaller than what's currently in my closet to give me a bigger incentive to stick with the diet and ignore how hungry I am.

Nescafe Diet Update: I am on day four of the diet and I have already lost three kilos. I'm sure it's mostly water, but it still feels fantastic, other than occasionally experiencing a slight dizziness that goes away after a few minutes. I am back down to 52 kilos and am hoping to reach 48 by the day of the party. I'm not even hungry anymore and feel quite energized and clearheaded. I won't lie—the first two days were horrible. I didn't really sleep the first night, that's how hungry I was. At least once I got out of bed and went as far as the kitchen before turning around and going back to bed.

I felt nauseous and really dizzy on the morning of the third day. I was on my way to the newsagent at the bottom of the street to get Mom her paper and some butter when suddenly the world turned grey. I seriously thought I was going to faint. I sat down on a nearby step, and after a few minutes the sensation passed, but I still felt very weak. When I returned home, I almost grabbed a banana out of the fruit bowl to stop me from shaking. It was inviting me to eat it, and I would have in about two bites, but I know myself. If I ate the banana, the magic of the diet would be gone and soon I'd be eating everything in sight. So, I walked right by it, ignoring the banana with my head held high! I am so proud of myself and my willpower.

I have no doubt I will get to my goal.

Nescafe Diet Final Update: Finally, it's finished. I didn't need ten days after all. I reached 48 kilos by day six. I'm especially glad about that, since Mom, even as dazed as she's been, was beginning to notice something wasn't right.

"It looks as if you lost a bit of weight," she commented. "It suits you. You haven't been skipping meals, have you?"

Of course, I denied it and blamed having less of an appetite on the summer heat, but I could tell she was onto me. Anyway, now it's done and all I have to do is be very careful with what I eat from now until the party, so I continue losing steadily. My new goal is 45 or even 43 kilos, but if Mom finds out she'll throw a fit, so I'm only sharing this information with Ginny.

Today I ate a banana, a chicken breast and two hard-boiled eggs with salad. Very healthy and less than 500 calories altogether. I'm definitely still hungry, but I have a secret weapon. Unshelled sunflower seeds. You can eat a whole bowl of them for only 150 calories. Unhulling them takes forever, so that occupies my mouth for hours and I don't feel deprived. Another secret is sesame seeds. I put a teaspoon of seeds on a little plate and then pluck them up one at a time. They have so much taste that I can feel each seed bursting with flavour as I bite into it. The risk here is they taste so good I will eat two or three at a time and finish too soon. In the past, I have gone back to the cupboard and got a second and third helping.

That will never do with the party coming up.

Chapter Fifteen

The Party

I am a pig! No doubt about it!

Yesterday was the day of the party. Ginny came over to my house three hours before the party to get ready. Both of us were faint from hunger, having dieted relentlessly for two weeks. I made us two iced Nescafe to take the edge off. My Greek friend Eleni turned me on to iced coffee and taught me how to make it properly. It's truly the perfect drink for a hot summer day.

Both Ginny and I pretty much knew what we were going to wear, but she came over with a suitcase full of clothes and makeup just in case she changed her mind at the last minute. Part of the fun of going to such a glamorous event is the preparation, and we certainly took full advantage of the time we had. I changed my nail polish twice to match my outfit. Ginny snuck a couple of beers into her bag, so we got a little tipsy and very giggly. Everything I tried on fit perfectly and I almost went for the low-slung trousers baring my midriff, but then I went back to my original pick which showed off my great legs.

Of all the parts of my body, I'm the proudest of my legs. They are long and flawless, other than the scar from when I fell of my bike chasing after my cousin Mike. Mom had to tweezer out a billion little stones and bits of gravel as I whimpered, not even wanting to look at the damage. It looks okay now, but I can still see the scar if I look closely. I also like my neck, which is long and graceful after many years of ballet. But I digress.

I ended up wearing a short black skirt made out of a shiny material which looked like leather, along with a red tank top. I had to buy both with my pocket money, as Mom would have refused to pay for anything like that. She would have thrown a fit if I'd even suggested it. But it looks fantastic, especially with my black boots and red nail polish. We had a bit of trouble getting out the door and past Mom's and Mamgu Winny's reproachful stares. Ever since I turned seventeen, both have given up telling me what to wear, but they have other ways of showing their dissatisfaction. I pretended not to notice and quickly left, with Ginny trying to catch up, teeter-tottering on her skyscraper heels.

I hadn't eaten anything since my light dinner the night before. The beer we'd drank earlier made me a bit dizzy, but in a happy kind of way. At the party, I had loads of admirers asking me to dance, and I felt really popular. I must have had three or four drinks in succession when I started feeling really sick. I sat quietly in a corner, hoping the effect would wear off—the sooner, the better. Through the blur, people kept coming and going, asking if I was okay and trying to move me. I wanted to go to the bathroom, but I was pretty sure if I moved, I would throw up, which was exactly what happened, right where I was, on Julie's mother's oriental carpet. It was so embarrassing and disgusting. I was mortified. An adult suddenly appeared. She cleaned up the whole mess and brought me a coffee and some bread to soak up the alcohol and settle my stomach. In my weakened state, I rationalized that I should probably eat the bread to make me feel better.

That was a huge mistake. As soon as I could move again, I made straight for the buffet and ate 10,000 calories. And I somehow managed that without anyone noticing. I would take a canape and pop it in my mouth, and then, holding two or three more, I'd go stand by the window and slyly eat the lot, partially hidden by the curtain. Then I'd go back for more, all the time wishing everyone away from me so that I would not be noticed or interrupted during my disgusting binge. I only stopped when Ginny found me to say that she was ready to leave. At that point, I had undone the top button of my skirt and the pleasant feeling of my clothes fitting perfectly had disappeared. My skirt was riding up, and you could clearly see my stomach rolls outlined by the tight tank top (which also by this time had a vomit stain across the front of it). I felt like an idiot and was happy to finally get home and change into my pyjamas.

I went straight to bed, but I couldn't sleep. I picked up a book, hoping to read, but something was missing. I shuffled downstairs for a snack and returned with a plate of leftover pasta. When I cleared my plate, I went back down for a second helping, including a hunk of cheese, a slice of cake, yogurt, and a packet of Oreos. I then googled how to make yourself throw up. I even went as far as to hug the toilet bowl and give it a try, but I was unsuccessful.

For the next two days I will not eat to make up for this dreadful performance.

PIG, PIG, PIG!

That's me.

Chapter Sixteen

A Day at the Beach

Today, Ginny and I took the train to the beach. I asked Rosie to join us, but she said she was busy. I'm guessing she didn't want to be seen in a swimsuit. I certainly wouldn't if I was as overweight as she is. I have a niggling thought in the back of my mind that she is avoiding me, but that can't be right. Perhaps she's just a bit jealous that I lost so much weight while she just keeps getting fatter and fatter.

Our diary has overstayed with me, as well. When we get back from the beach, I will write something and hand it over to her for her turn. The reason I've not done it so far is that I'm interested in different things than she is, and I don't think Rosie would care or even understand what I want to write about.

Today we went to the beach farthest away from our town. I've been to this beach a million times, but never without an adult. It felt wonderful to be trusted, and although I was a bit nervous, I was hugely excited. Ginny's mom is very liberal. Ginny has been going on trains on her own since the beginning of secondary school.

On the train, she barely spoke to me. Sitting by the window, she whispered on her phone while tugging at the hole in her tights. As the hole got bigger and bigger, she started twisting it into a knot. Despite myself, I found it mesmerizing to watch. She looked incredibly grown up and sexy, and I wished I was like her. I felt very childish in my shorts and oversized T-shirt. I wish I had picked something more sophisticated to wear—although not going as far as black tights. Even with the holes she made, they made her look super-hot.

The ride to the beach is only an hour, but when the trolley came by, she asked for a Coke, a Kit Kat bar and a packet of M&Ms. I'm not one for a healthy breakfast, but I was surprised to see her gobbling down the whole lot while staring at her phone. She offered to share, but I'm not eating anything today, thank you very much. It's easier to fast when I'm not at home with Mom watching my every move. I had already given up my packed lunch to a homeless guy outside the station in order to remove any temptation. As soon as the last M&M disappeared, Ginny got up and headed for the bathroom.

She came back visibly paler and sat down next to me. I caught a whiff of sick on her, thinly disguised by her peppermint gum.

"How can you eat all this crap and stay skinny?" I demanded.

Ginny waved my question away.

"You know you can eat anything you want if you throw it up within ten minutes."

Yuck! I couldn't believe she just said that.

"Don't look so shocked. Everybody does it. Just carry some gum and no one will know." I left it at that, but the wheels in my brain were spinning. Perhaps it would work and be worth a try, but the gum didn't really cover the smell of the vomit. I told her that, but she just made a face at me.

"It goes away quickly. Don't worry about it."

Once we were at the beach, we spread our towels—hers with a pink ice cream pattern and mine with colourful stripes—and went to the changing rooms. Ginny came out wearing a skimpy bikini which perfectly matched her beach towel. I had a bikini in my bag but chose to wear my one-piece instead. Ginny is so thin that if I stood next to her in a bikini I'd look like a lumpy bag of potatoes.

"Let's go for a walk and see if there are any cute guys," she suggested, pulling a pack of cigarettes from her bag. Ginny always has cigarettes on her. She looks older than the rest of us, so she can get them at most newsagents when she's not wearing school uniform. She offered me one and I happily took it. I am not an experienced smoker, mostly because I can't always buy my own cigarettes the way Ginny can, but also because I'm afraid Mom will sniff me out. I can't hide from her, and even though it gets annoying at times, I am mostly glad we are so close.

Soon Ginny and I were walking together by the surf, puffing on our ciggies. I felt ten feet tall and super cool. I was sure all eyes were on us, but I pretended I didn't notice. I looked straight ahead, listening to Ginny talk about this and that.

At lunchtime, after a morning of swimming, and having eaten nothing since last night, I started regretting giving my lunch away. I was so hungry. All the cafes on the beach were full of people eating mountains of shiny fries and juicy burgers. Of course, they were all overweight, with rolls of fat spilling out of their swimsuits.

I really don't mind fat people, and I never criticize anyone for being overweight. Some people just can't help themselves or they don't have the discipline to say no when they see food. I get that. It's their choice.

My choice is to stay thin and feel good about myself and the way I look. Feeling very superior and also quite virtuous for not having eaten anything all day, I walked past the row of cafes. We reached the end of the beach, and right there, hidden by the forest of umbrellas, was a lonely cafe calling out my name...

I don't know who that girl was who went up to the counter and ordered a monstrously large basket of fries. It couldn't possibly have been me. I am a strong, confident woman who is in control of her eating. Holding the steaming basket in my hands, I resolved I would only eat three fries and throw out the rest.

I offered the basket to Ginny, but she opted instead for another cigarette. This made me feel even more guilty as I stared down at the greasy French fries. I mentally counted the calories. There were probably twenty calories in each fry. I started by slowly chewing on the first one, hoping to make it last as long as possible.

Then something awful overtook me! An incredible, unstoppable hunger I couldn't control. I couldn't make myself slow down or stop. I walked over to the bin, determined to throw out the lot.

Instead, I just stood over the trash can like an idiot, stuffing my face as quickly as possible, partially hidden by the side of the cafe. Still holding the last fry, I went back to the counter and got two slices of pizza and then an ice cream. I hated myself for every second of it.

Why am I so weak?

I really am a pig.

All my work dieting from last week totally wasted. I am sure I gained a kilo or more. I started counting the calories and came up with at least 1,200. I felt sick about it and wanted to go home.

Ginny was having none of it.

"Right. Follow me!" she instructed firmly, leading the way to the toilets. She pushed me into the farthest cubicle and shut the door behind us. I knew what she wanted me to do.

"It's no use. I've never managed to get myself to throw up," I said. "I even watched a video on YouTube, but it's impossible for me."

She scoffed and pulled a toothbrush out of her bag, handing it to me.

"Put the back side of this in your mouth and touch your tongue as far back as you can," she instructed. After several tries and lots of gagging, I finally found success! I felt so proud of myself. Watching the half-digested fries being flushed away made me feel so strong and in control of myself. I was the master of my fate, and I had a new skill to solve my biggest problem! I was so grateful to Ginny.

She is an amazing friend.

Chapter Seventeen

A Garden by the River
(The Day We Lost Our Ball)

I don't get to see my two cousins very often because they live a day's journey away from us. Sometimes they visit at Christmas, but not very often. I know Dad misses his brother, but he's really not very fond of Aunt Emily. When he thinks we're not listening, he calls her *Ice on Heels*. She definitely deserves the title. Unfortunately for her, she never made it to royalty, and everyone has to suffer because of it. Every time our families get together, she supposedly *throws out her back* to avoid hanging out with Mom, whom she envies in a passive-aggressive way. Mom, being Mom, doesn't give a hoot how Aunt Emily feels about her and this annoys Aunt Emily to no end.

This year, Dad and his brother agreed to surprise Mamgu Winny and Emily's mom Elizabeth, and rent a big house by the sea for the two families to spend a week together in. The house was quite spectacular, with a large lawn right on the river estuary. Despite the on-and-off rain, the adults stubbornly insisted on shivering on sun loungers, cocktails in one hand and thermal blankets in another, all the while avoiding contentious subjects.

Aunt Emily loves to cook. Even though we were on vacation, she prepared two elaborate meals every day, and left the cleaning up for us kids to do. For me, of course, this is double punishment, as I had to sit at the table twice a day picking at the salad in front of me, and then I had to spend an hour clearing the table and doing the dishes. Aunt Emily is a messy cook, who also pretends to be a chef. Nobody has the heart to tell her that many of her creations leave both the kids and adults unimpressed, but the sheer amount of pots, pans and dishes she always uses makes me wish someone would.

I was a bit nervous, because there wasn't any scales in the house, and I couldn't tell what was happening on the weight front. I've been pretty good this week, but I did on occasion fall off the wagon.

Dishes and scales aside, us kids had a terrific time. Ella and I love our cousins and even agreed to ignore the weather and take part in a dodgeball tournament with our youngest cousin Mike, who is only seven. His sister Jean is close to my age, and even though she agreed to play, I could tell she was dying to sit near the adults and play on her phone.

I was coming back from the bathroom when my cousin Mike burst into the cottage and fell in his mother's lap, sobbing uncontrollably.

"Mom, Mom, my ball is gone," he wailed. Emily looked out the window just in time to catch a quick glimpse of the fast-disappearing red Arsenal ball. A high kick had sent it over the fence and into the river where the outgoing tide rapidly swept the ball towards the estuary.

"Looks like a fabulous opportunity for a rescue mission," Aunt Emily declared to the slightly bored crowd gathered around the table. Three days of constant rain had dampened everyone's spirits, but the promise of a high-seas ball rescue brought a few cheers.

Grandparents, parents, children, and the dog filed out into the sodden garden to assess the situation. Mike, pleased by the response, had forgotten his despair and was running up and down the length of the riverside fence, gesturing enthusiastically toward the river. Options were quickly discussed, including convincing the dog to swim after the ball, sending out a kid with a rope around his or her waist, or borrowing what appeared to be an abandoned surfboard.

As negotiations progressed, Mike and Jean lost interest in the rescue mission and retreated into the dry coziness of the cottage. The dog, fearing the increasing probability of personal involvement in the operation, quickly followed in their wake. This left six soaked adults and Ella and me staring towards the bobbing red ball.

Suddenly in the distance, a rowboat appeared. All six adults started screaming and gesturing at the same time. The rowers waved back enthusiastically. The shore-based party pointed towards the ball. The rowers pointed towards the mouth of the river and gave a thumbs up. The shore-based party increased the intensity of the gesturing and the rowers reciprocated. The rain continued to pelt everyone. It was crazy.

Emily quickly surveyed the situation and came to a decision.

"Let's have a cup of tea. I'll get Mike a new ball this afternoon." Everyone cheered. The rowers cheered back.

The next day we got a new ball.

Chapter Eighteen

A Villa in the Sun

Finally, we came to the best part of summer. Mom and Dad save all year for our week in the sun. This year we were going to Greece to a resort in Kalamata. I was surprised to find out that Kalamata olives are named after an actual city in Greece. The whole family has been reading up on the area, while I have mostly been lying in the garden in my bikini, hoping to catch some rays. I read on the Internet that you can get a tan even when it's overcast outside, but I don't believe it anymore. Despite lying there and getting through the entirety of *Pride and Prejudice*, I am still as pale as a dead fish.

I think being pale is one of the things people find hardest to understand and accept. I am constantly reminded by random people that I am so tall, that my hair is so red and that I am so pale. As strange as it may seem, I am fully aware of my skin and hair colour, and I am sick to death of never being allowed to forget it! I've had it all my life, after all. Rant over!

I have been packing for weeks. We are each allowed a suitcase up to 23 kilos, but because it costs extra per suitcase, Mom and Dad are sharing one, and for the first time ever, I am being allowed to have my own checked luggage. I found a website which sells bikinis for a tenner, and I bought several. Unfortunately, only half have arrived, and nobody is answering my increasingly desperate emails. I've packed several sundresses, shorts, and loads of tops. I also packed a pair of pink shorts that's too small for me to wear right now, but I plan to lose at least two kilos while we're in Kalamata. It will be sort of a challenge for me. I've packed my diet pills and a few laxatives to help me along. Of course, laxatives don't help me lose weight. Not really. But they give me a wonderful feeling of emptiness, and my belly gets pretty flat, even if I overeat.

With Ginny's encouragement and a VERY strict diet, I am down three kilos despite my occasional binges. I would like to get down to 42 kilos, but it is looking unlikely in the very short time before we leave. Ginny and I did a 1,000 crunches challenge, which I easily won. She got bored halfway through the challenge and left to meet her other friends for coffee. I was a bit upset that she didn't ask me to come along, but then again, I was also proud of myself for finishing the challenge—with or without her.

We flew EasyJet to Greece, and we all had to sit in separate parts of the plane. I didn't mind, as I wrote in my diary the whole way there. I try to stay on track with what I eat by writing about my feelings and all the great things that will happen to me when I lose weight. I was thinking about starting a blog about my weight struggles. I might even get a small following to help me reach my goal. I may use this holiday to plan it.

The flight is almost four hours, so I had time to write about Mom and Dad as well. This is the first vacation ever where Mom has been indifferent about our week in the sun. Normally, she runs around excitedly packing this and that while worrying about Mamgu Winny and organizing her daily commute to the shop. This year, she seemed almost depressed to have to go. I told Ella to give Mom and Dad space to talk while we are in Kalamata, and I will do the same.

The villa is amazing, and it has its own pool. Not a very big pool, mind you, but perfect for cooling down after a session of sunbathing. Ella and I are sharing a room, and Mom and Dad took the bedroom with the sea view. It didn't take long before we met loads of kids from neighbouring villas, and we were in the sea before we even unpacked. I will lose three kilos, meet a gorgeous new guy and get a tan, and Mom and Dad will solve all of their problems!

I have a great feeling about this holiday.

Chapter Nineteen

A Villa in the Sun
Part Two

Nothing goes as expected, and neither did this holiday. I gained a kilo, I met a local guy who tried to steal my iPhone, I have an angry sunburn all over my body, and Dad spent most of the week on his iPad (but at least I didn't hear much in the way of arguments). I thought being away from home and with Mom not cooking it would be easy to reach my weight goal. How wrong I was.

Eating out every day proved to be my undoing. I thought I was doing well just ordering a Greek salad every day, but at the bottom of the plate I always found a wonderful mix of olive oil, feta crumbles, and vinegar which I scooped up with half a loaf of bread. Halfway through the week, nothing in my suitcase fit comfortably anymore and I ended up wearing the same sundress Mom bought me from a beach vendor. Of course, I deserved it. I have zero willpower and I didn't even bother to exercise, other than to lazily flop in the shallows like the blubbery seal I will end up looking like.

I am a PIG. It has now been decided for real.

Something fun actually happened, but I am not totally sure it was meant that way. I had sex for the first time with the guy who tried to steal my iPhone. In truth, it was a bit of a non-event and nothing like the profound and meaningful experience I thought it would be. We were at a local disco with a large group of kids and he asked me to dance. We'd had a bit to drink, as nobody cares about IDs in Kalamata. Then he started kissing me and led me towards the beach. And it was on the beach, behind a fishing boat, that Winny Stokes became a woman.

It was nothing at all like I expected. Firstly, it didn't hurt at all. There was no blood. And it lasted less than two minutes. I mean, really? I didn't feel good or bad about it, either way. It was actually a bit boring. He made lots of funny noises and I joined in so that he would not get offended, if you can even imagine. How funny is that? When it was finished, he laid there for a bit smoking a cigarette. He gave me one, too. Then, as he was putting his clothes on, I noticed him reaching for my jacket where I had my iPhone. I jumped up, grabbed it out of his hands and ran back to meet the others at the disco. Not very glamorous, eh? At least I am not a virgin anymore, but I am terrified for a whole different reason. I didn't even remember to ask him if he had a condom! I hope I didn't catch anything or get pregnant.

Poor Mom. This is how she found out what happened. At 3 a.m., she walked into the bathroom as I was staring blankly at the mirror. She asked me what I was looking at, and without thinking, I told her I'd become a woman and was looking to see if I'd changed. As you can imagine, this conversation quickly unraveled into a mixture of accusations, tears, and warnings. Ella woke up and came to see what the fuss was about, and soon the entire Stokes family knew I'd had SEX for the first time with a random guy on a Greek beach.

Peachy!

Chapter Twenty

Back On My Horse

I may be fat, but at least I'm not pregnant, and it appears I didn't catch any terrible disease either, thankfully. But now that I'm back, there is no excuse left for me. The weight has to go. I'm not going to go out and buy a whole new wardrobe and look like a rhinoceros when I go back to school. On the flight back from Greece, I wrote in my diary my new diet plan.

It's the strictest one ever, I'm going to follow it for sure! I have no other choice. I refused the meal on the plane, even though it was lunchtime. I decided to eat NOTHING for three days. I gobbled up six diet pills and a laxative for good measure. If I had thought about it, I could have waited until we got home before pulling a stunt like that, but in the midst of my self-loathing and severe resolutions, I didn't.

As a result, I spent the whole train ride home in the toilet, with people banging on the door wanting to come in. Finally, Mom came to the door with the conductor and I had to admit to my problem with the entire train listening. It was so embarrassing. I refused to come out of the bathroom until we reached the station, no matter what. At home, I ran straight for the scales, where I was happily rewarded for my suffering.

I was the same weight as before we left for Greece!

Chapter Twenty-One

A Fine Day to Run

Summer is almost finished, and I am feeling nervous about going back to school, but I'm also feeling quite good about my new figure. Perfecting Ginny's trick has changed my life, and for the first time I feel in charge of my weight. I am so good at throwing up now, I can do it in less than a minute and be back from the bathroom before anyone suspects a thing.

Today, we walked with Mom to the bus stop. Since early summer, she has been more and more distracted, and the arguments filtering up to my bedroom more often than not end up with her sobbing loudly enough for me to hear. During our week in Greece, things appeared to be improving, but now that we're back, it's worse than before. She's being quite secretive about what's going on, but I can tell things are not okay. Her routine has changed, and she seems more worried about money than usual.

As the bus pulled away, I saw her looking quite worried and typing something on her phone. I sure hope she works things out with Dad. I don't want to be one of those kids whose parents argue all the time. I switched on my iPod, took a quick look at my laces to make sure they were tight and started my usual 5K morning run. Picking up speed, I headed for the riverfront.

It was still quite dark, but the glow of the predawn was visible over the city buildings. I know this route with my eyes closed. Rarely do I meet anyone in those solitary runs, and I like it that way. Yesterday it was raining, but this morning it was clear and crisp. As I ran, I started feeling warmer and more comfortable. The new development slipped by as my confidence and wellbeing grew.

From the corner of my eye, I saw a sailboat go by. I vaguely waved in its direction. A solitary figure at the wheel waved back. The tide was going out and I could hear waves splashing against the ancient river pilings. I jumped into my head and searched for happy thoughts. Little buds appeared one by one. As I put one foot in front of the other, I let the buds flower, picking those I liked best. I was in a fine mood.

An old ankle injury briefly interrupted my daydream with a dull pang. I ignored it. The sun was now warming my back. It would be in my eyes on the way back. I quick glanced behind me. No one was there. Ahead, a small figure rushed towards me. Female, I decided. High heels, swinging briefcase, purposefully walking toward the tube station. There would be many others behind her, as the city was beginning to wake. I reached the red bridge. Time to start heading back. I blinked at the sun and smiled.

It was going to be a fine day.

Chapter Twenty-Two

Mirrors

I don't know what to think about mirrors. We have many at home and they mostly make me feel very anxious. I look at myself in the mirror probably every half hour. I know that sounds like an awful lot, but I also count the times I just look at my face or the times I catch a quick glimpse as I'm walking by.

I've noticed most mirrors make you look fatter or thinner. I find both types to be a problem. I have often bought something at a shop with a thinning mirror only to find out when I get home that what I've purchased actually makes me look fat. At home, I can mostly tell which of the mirrors are lying. We even have a mirror that lies both ways—half of it makes you look fat and the other half thin. I always make sure I stand on the thin side so as not to get depressed.

My favourite reflection is the one I see in window panes on the street. It is vague enough so I can replace it with what I would like to look like. I try not to be too obvious when I do that, so it's always no more than a fleeting image. Sometimes it can get embarrassing if you find someone looking back at you from inside the building, so I try to be quick and discreet.

The best way to check if a mirror is accurate is to get someone to stand next to you and compare what you see in the mirror with the way they look in person. I try to do that in my exercise class at the gym at school, but it's really hard because I have to stand right next to them, and that can get a bit weird and awkward. Ella is the only person who is happy to play the game with me, but she refuses to take her clothes off or to wear something tight, so it's impossible to use her as a model.

Another thing that can make a huge difference is the light. If it's harsh daylight, I can see clearly the bits of me I really hate, like the fat above my knees and my fat belly. When I lie in bed and suck it in, it feels all right, but as soon as I get up, everything spills out like a disgusting blobby fat tyre. Ginny thinks what I'm seeing is muscle, but I know it's ugly fat that just won't go away unless I cut down on the bread and the crisps.

I've also been experimenting with camera angles. If a picture is taken from high up, I look a lot thinner and my B-cup boobs look a lot bigger. I decided to order a selfie stick so I can experiment all I want without bothering Ella. Then I can try some pictures in my underwear to see if I can look really skinny. It would be too weird to get Ella to do that. If they end up looking all right, I can use them as motivational pictures.

I started a new Instagram account, separate from my regular account. It's dedicated to dieting and being thin. I already have 79 followers after only two weeks. I haven't posted any pictures of me yet, but if I manage to find the right angle, I may post one.

Not showing my face, obviously.

Chapter Twenty-Three

Nescafe Diet:
Take Two

There are two weeks to go before school starts and I want to look amazing, so I've decided to have another few days on the Nescafe diet. I am now 45 kilos, but I want to lose a couple more. This time it didn't go as well as before. Two evenings in a row, I ended up in front of the fridge at midnight, and once I didn't even bother fixing the problem with a quick bathroom visit. I was also worried that Mom was beginning to figure out what I was up to. I felt I had to hide from her. I had taken to wearing loose clothes around the house, but I caught her more than once staring at me intently.

Then it happened.

As I was hugging the toilet bowl after gorging on mom's lasagna, she burst into the bathroom. I was found out. Stupidly, in my haste, I had forgotten to lock the door. She turned as white as a sheet, picked me up, and hugged me tightly.

"How long have you been doing this?" she demanded to know.

"It's not what you think," I told her. "I just felt nauseous. I have a stomach virus and the lasagna made it worse," I lied.

But she was on to me. She pulled out the scale from under the sink and made me stand on it. If it was possible, her face lost even more colour. I was 43 kilos. Despite what just happened, I could not suppress a smile.

Success!

First thing the next morning, she took me to the GP, having managed to arrange an emergency appointment. Nothing I said registered—not the tears, not the pleading, not the promises.

"You have a problem and we are going to solve it," was all she would say. I was referred to group therapy on the spot.

Things were looking bleak.

Chapter Twenty-Four

Therapy

"I will treat you like an adult," Mom promised, "but you will have to go to therapy and I will watch your weight. If it drops any further, I will start treating you like a child. Deal?" What could I say, other than to agree with her terms?

Therapy wasn't that bad. It was twice a week for three hours, with a short break for refreshments. Cookies and cakes were piled up high on tables and we were encouraged to get up and have one whenever we wanted. I met everyone on the first day. All of us were girls between the ages of twelve and eighteen. Some of the girls were super thin and I was quite jealous. I think I was the chunkiest in the group. I would like to have been more like some of the thinner girls, but it's looking difficult now that Mom is on to me.

The leader was a guy in his thirties, or maybe a bit older. He had a soothing way about him, not at all teacher-like. I liked him right away, even though he wanted to make me fat. I was there because Mom made me go, not to gain weight. I think all the other girls felt the same way, and we talked about it during the breaks.

They had lots of tricks to teach me, including drinking lots of water before Mom weighed me, or filling my pockets with weights. One of the girls had discovered an amazing concealer for dark circles and makeup tricks to make your face look fuller and avoid parental scrutiny. Talking to them, I felt hopeful that I could escape any attempts to derail my diet.

Most of the therapy involved us talking about why we want to be thin, and also about our families, school etc. I told him what he wanted to hear and pretended to be horrified by the risks of extreme dieting. But I don't really believe him.

I feel great, and so do the others in my group.

AUTUMN

Chapter Twenty-Five

Back to School

Finally, school started. I never thought I'd be so happy to go back to school and face homework, but being at home had become suffocating. Mom is micromanaging everything I do, particularly what I eat and drink. I've avoided turning into a cow so far, but to do that I've had to go to great lengths to deceive her, and I don't like that. I found putting Ella's juggling sand-filled balls into my pockets and drinking a litre of water work quite effectively come weigh-in time.

I have managed to take off another kilo without her suspecting a thing. She even agreed to let me stop therapy, as it interferes with my study time. She was clear, though, that I must have regular meals, empty my plate and keep my weight stable or I would have to go back.

This is my final exam year and I'm taking some pretty hard subjects. Chemistry is the hardest, but I've also chosen maths, history, and physics. Ginny thinks I'm crazy, but I'm not worried. I've always found school easy and I have great plans for university. She's picked all the easy subjects, and even though she says she hasn't decided yet, I don't think university is in her future plans. Certainly not with subjects such as drama, art, and photography.

She wants to be a model, find a rich husband, and enjoy her life on yachts and exotic vacations. She is very pretty, tall, and quite thin, so that's not an impossible dream for her. I hope we can stay friends, as I'll not have much time for parties and going out now that school has started. It's only the first week and I'm already buried in homework.

It was really great to be with my friend group again. I didn't see much of anyone over the summer, other than Ginny. They were all amazed by how thin I am. Hannah also lost some weight and it really suits her. For the last year of school, we will all be super busy, but there will also be lots of eighteenth birthday parties to attend. The big news is that Megan also had sex for the first time. Now three of us have done it—and all three of us agree it's overrated.

I'm certainly not going to be doing it with James. That relationship is probably over. I didn't see him or miss him at all during the summer. Megan's boyfriend is halfway across the world in Australia. And as for Ginny, she is never with anyone long enough for us to meet. She says that as soon as a boyfriend starts getting clingy, she stops liking them. Mom says that is normal at our age because we are still growing, and our tastes change all the time.

Lila and Hannah became a lot closer this summer because they went to Hannah's summer home together. I'm a little upset that I wasn't invited, and I feel excluded when they talk about what they did and the people they met. Hannah's parents have an amazing villa in Majorca with a pool and a hot tub. I saw their Instagram photos, posing together at the edge of the pool and in front of giant paella pans, and I wished I was there with them—but not eating the paella, of course. It looked incredibly fattening.

I wonder if we will all be as close as we were before the summer or whether our group will break in two. I am certainly much closer to Ginny now, and poor Megan is a bit like the odd one out. I made a point of asking her all sorts of questions about her summer in Australia and her new boyfriend, but she didn't want to say much. I know Megan had been secretly wishing she could spend the summer doing things with her dad. She missed him a lot. But it sounds as if she barely saw him the entire summer. I think her dad must have been too preoccupied with his new family and sort of ignored her. I can't imagine what it would feel like for your dad to behave like a stranger.

Speaking of dads, Dad is away a lot! I think he is trying to avoid arguments and the problems at home (although I'm the main problem, I guess). It's not as if he is staying in any glamorous locations, and he claims to hate all the extra overnight trips, but he isn't fooling anyone, least of all Mom, who is raising her voice more often than ever before. When he's away, she has to take care of everything, including his mum. But mostly I am beginning to think she is worried. Of course, I don't believe Dad would have a girlfriend. He isn't the type to cheat.

But I wish he'd stick around more and make Mom feel more secure.

Chapter Twenty-Six

My Love Life Has to Get Better

James was away all last summer, and when we finally saw each other at school, it was clear things had changed. He did make some feeble attempts to kiss me during break, but we could both tell the feelings were no longer there. I suppose this happens often with people our age.

Our relationship seemed so childish now that I've had sex. I'm sure he is still a virgin, even though he claims he has done it before. Per my usual way of breaking up, I said nothing to him about breaking up. I just suddenly became really busy and unavailable. He stopped calling more quickly than I expected, and that stung a bit, but I was glad to be rid of him.

With my new figure, I look better than ever, and there is a new guy at school who has caught my eye. Mark is a friend of a friend at my maths tutoring school. I don't think he has a girlfriend, and I have often caught him looking at me during class. He looks like the sort of guy who would not be satisfied with above-the-waist stuff, so I am keeping my options open for now.

With all of us going somewhere different at the end of this year, the general consensus is to avoid any serious attachments. In fact, most couples seem to be breaking up before circumstances do it for them. There is the prom to worry about, of course, but it's months away, and many things can change before then.

Like my weight.

Chapter Twenty-Seven

My Jeans Don't Fit

I have been eating again. Mom stopped with the weigh-ins a while back. I have been emptying my plate, snacking while studying, and most days, taking a slice of the cake which always seems to be on the counter. Without a boyfriend, and with endless study sessions and Mom's delicious cooking, the kilos must have crept on. I realized that I've been avoiding many things in my wardrobe. The great judge of where I am on the piglet scale is the pair of jeans I bought last summer. I pulled them out of the bottom of the closet, and even before I put them on, I realized they wouldn't go past my knees. They were not just too tight. They were two sizes too small!

I'm not surprised, of course. Getting fat is a slippery slope and it's happened to me before. The weight slowly comes back on, and even though I know it, I avoid the scales out of fear of what they are going to show. Yes, I have done this before. I ran to the bathroom to weigh myself, but the scales were gone. Mom had probably hidden them or thrown them out. Panic gripped me and my heart started racing. I threw on some clothes and tumbled down the hill to the pharmacy. Standing in front of the upright scales, I took off my shoes, socks, and anything else I could take off without offending our chemist, who's known me since I was a baby. I mentally calculated the weight of the clothes I still had on, took a deep breath and stepped on. Fifty kilos! I had gained almost eight kilos!

How can that be? Is it even physically possible?

I looked in the mirror in front of me and I saw a giant whale looking back at me. I'd tried so hard to love my body, but how can I love this? Once I got home, I flicked through my Facebook pictures from when I was skinny, and I missed it terribly, despite all the purging and being cold all the time. I'd been beautiful then, and now I just don't feel that way. I'm so uncomfortable in my body.

Then and there, I took a vow to eat nothing for at least a week. I would need to figure out what to do so Mom wouldn't notice, but it would probably be okay. She didn't appear to be watching me that closely anymore, and the constantly worried look during mealtimes had left her face. I wondered if it was safe to walk to the chemist down the street to stock up on supplies but decided against it. The chemist knows us quite well and he would probably tell Mom.

Instead, I chose a pharmacy further away, and stocked up on diet pills, diuretics, and laxatives. First of all, though, I had to find out the real damage. How much of this was last night's meal of four-cheese tortellini, bananas, nuts, and chocolate cake? I tried to remember when I had my last period, which always adds half a kilo of weight or more. Since the Nescafe Diet, my periods had been sporadic and unpredictable, so I put that thought aside. I swallowed some of the pills as I walked home.

After drinking four glasses of water, everything started coming out. I felt so much better. It was as if I was getting rid of poisonous fat. Of course, I know that it wasn't fat, not yet, but it still felt good. I ran back down to the chemist and got on the scales again. A whole kilo had disappeared.

I call this a good start.

Chapter Twenty-Eight

Undercover on the Nescafe Diet

I thought this would be a lot harder than it turned out to be. Mom isn't watching anymore. Her eyes are often red and irritated, and she leaves her sentences unfinished, forgetting what she was saying. She has certainly lost a lot of weight, and it's making her look older and a bit grey. Dad has too, but in his case, it really suits him. He bought a bench and weights, and he spends a half-hour every morning working out. His overnight trips are now twice a week, and when he is at home, he sits on the leather chair away from the rest of us, deeply interested in whatever is on his iPad. Every now and then, he chuckles and smiles, but he never shares the jokes with us like he used to.

He seems to be in his own world. Ella has been trying to get him to fix the flat tyre on her bike for weeks without luck. Now that I think about it, he hasn't asked me anything about school since I started, which is totally out of character for him. He's always been interested in what's happening at school. I wonder if he's even noticed I've got fat.

The upside of all this, of course, is that nobody has noticed my frequent bathroom visits. I figured it was easier and safer to eat with the family and then purge everything in the usual way. To throw Mom off the scent, I've varied my visits, sometimes going in the middle of the meal, while other times at the end. My latest trick was getting Ginny to call me, so I had to run upstairs to talk to her without raising suspicion. At school, I got my meals as usual, so the charge appeared on my Uniware card, and then I'd either give it to whoever wanted it or discretely throw it in the bin. I don't think anyone was watching, but I wanted to be safe and cautious in my movements.

The weight started dropping quickly, and soon I could pull up my jeans. I felt very happy and energetic despite the lack of food. I would lie in my bed at night stroking my flat belly, gently touching my hip bones where they tugged against the skin. I also got back into running again. Exercise had also fallen by the wayside as the weight piled on. But soon, I could run every day, almost effortlessly. As the pounds dropped, I started running twice a day, and I also walked everywhere instead of taking the bus. I was unstoppable!

This time it was Mamgu Winny who caught me in the act. Her eyes are not that old, after all. It turned out she'd been carefully watching me. She said she'd noticed the change on my face and that I'd been wearing loose tracksuits and bulky tops while at home. One day during dinner, when Ginny called mid-meal and I disappeared into the living room, she silently followed me and caught me retching in the bathroom. I had become careless and stopped going upstairs. That was my mistake. Mamgu Winny is slow and noisy on the staircase, and I would have heard her coming, but she is quick and nimble on her feet on even, level ground.

When I was discovered, everyone joined in the furore. Even Dad looked up from his iPad and joined in the recriminations—and believe me, there was plenty of those. Even Ella joined in with a dose of tears and hysterics. I know they were worried, but this was way over the top. I was still a healthy weight at 45 kilos, and was three kilos above my lowest weight.

Clearly my whole family wanted to see me fat!

Chapter Twenty-Nine

Therapy:
Take Two

The GP decided that Mom would be in charge of what I eat,
and I had to go to back to group therapy. I decided the best
strategy was to go along with whatever they suggested to
stop her from whining. She is stressed enough as it is, and
I'm really worried that whatever is going on with Mom and
Dad is quite serious. No therapy will make me fat again, of
that I am sure, but it's a major hassle regardless. The meeting
is once a week after school at St. George's Trust. Last time
there was six of us—all girls. I recognized a few of the faces
from last time. Some of the girls were quite a bit thinner than
me.

One super-skinny girl sat next to me. Suddenly I felt very
fat and that I needed to lose more weight. She smiled at me.

"You are looking good," she said. Now I was sure I
looked fat. She told me that keeping the weight off was quite
a struggle with her mom watching her every move all the
time. Everyone here is afraid of being force-fed, but when I

read up on it, it appeared very unlikely that it would ever happen without the person agreeing, and nobody in this group had ever been force-fed or knew anyone who had. I also asked my thinness forum, and they hadn't heard of any cases either. I googled force-feeding when I got home and there were very few cases. Back in the day, the government force-fed the protesting suffragettes and caused permanent injuries to some of them. I think if I were ever going to protest about anything, I would also use dieting as my protest of choice.

Even though force-feeding looked unlikely, we all wanted to get our parents off our backs. Many of the girls had some amazing tips and tricks to share. My favourite, which I plan to try, is sewing weights into trousers. My mom does all my laundry, so I would have to make sure that I wash them separately. On second thought, Mom would probably notice that she never washed that particular pair. She's really very observant when it comes to me and Ella, especially now. One of the girls says she keeps her nails really long so when her mom gives her toast with cream cheese or butter she can scoop as much as possible under her nails without her mom noticing. Yuck! I think that she's disturbed and should definitely be in therapy.

The meeting went as expected, with the group leader going through all of the horrible health effects we were bringing upon ourselves, including infertility, bone loss, and potential death, blah, blah, blah.

When he left, we all agreed that he was probably exaggerating, and even if he wasn't, none of us cared. Being thin is all that matters.

Watch me shrink.
I'll prove it to everyone.
I won't stop until I'm tiny.
I will be thin.

Chapter Thirty

Lonely

I think our friendship group is breaking apart. Since the beginning of term, Hannah and Lila have been hanging out together and have become close with other girls at school. Megan seems to be totally absorbed with a guy she met at a party, and Ginny hasn't returned my messages for ages. I feel isolated, and I am beginning to think they are avoiding me. When I run into them at school, they look at me with this annoyingly sad look in their faces, as if I'm sick. I wonder if it's because I'm in therapy. I don't really know how to broach the subject with them without making it sound like it's a big deal, which it totally isn't, because therapy is a bit of a joke. Anyway, all of them have questionable eating habits as well, so it can't be that.

Some of this is my fault for sure. I've been avoiding events where food is involved. I try to stay away from temptation. Instead, I propose other activities such as exercising or shopping. I don't really like sitting around a table for hours pretending to eat while I am trying to diet. I cancel last minute. I prefer to be on my own, I don't have the mental energy to be around people.

I was never the one with a big group of friends behind me. I only have my friendship group and Rosie, who I have known since I was little. The thing is, I suck at maintaining friendships—I can go weeks without talking to or hanging out with my friends. Since the beginning of this year, I've been best when isolating myself and avoiding social situations. Sometimes even going to school takes a lot of effort.

I really have no idea how to make new friends. I don't trust myself and always think people believe the worst of me. I constantly feel stupid and annoying to others, so why bother? I have nothing to offer. I'm way too complicated sometimes and hate explaining myself. Whenever someone messages or calls me, I panic. I don't want to be like this for the rest of my life though. How the hell can one live like that?

I'm not weighing myself. The scales are in the bathroom, and it's a struggle every morning, deciding whether to look or not. I don't want to know. I know that I'm not even close to my all-time low weight, so I'll hate myself even more if I look. I'm scared to look. But I'm dying to know.

I hate myself.

Chapter Thirty-One

An Accident

Yesterday I went for my self-imposed longest run of the week (15K). I left the house at 5 a.m. to avoid any interrogation. It was dark and I was running on uneven pavement. Not surprisingly, I tripped and fell really hard. I got back up and looked at my phone. I was only at 7K. I limped down the trail, and all I could think was, "I have to run eight more kilometres!"

So, I did.

When I got home, having reached 15K, my knee was bloody and swollen. There was blood on my other leg as well, and I was bleeding from my chin and hand. One side of my body was covered in dirt. My knee hurt for days, but it didn't stop me from exercising. I did crunches and squats instead.

When I told Ginny at school, she thought I was crazy.

Funny, coming from her!

Chapter Thirty-Two

A Day at the Hair Salon

The day came to cut my hair. Mom made the appointment a month ago. Danielle's is our family hairdresser. Her salon is a few blocks from our house, located next to the newsagent. When Mom made my appointment, I fully expected it to be cancelled because it was nearing the time Danielle was due to give birth. Nobody, including her, thought she would still be cutting hair at eight months pregnant, but as I walked in, there she was, as chipper and energetic as ever. Wearing ballet pumps, trendy clothes, and sporting a huge belly which was initially hidden by the client on the black swivel chair, she greeted me enthusiastically. To be honest, I was relieved, as I don't really trust her assistant. Recently my hair has been looking rather thin and lifeless and I'm hoping she knows how to fix this.

The salon is a bright, tiny room with two stations. Danielle wants to know how short I want it cut. I show her the magazine I brought with me. She agrees this style would look good on me and would suit my hair type. While the assistant washes my hair, Danielle waddles the length of the salon, sits for a moment, and is quickly on her feet again. I marvel at the size of her belly and her ability to stand upright for any length of time as she concludes a quick phone call.

Hair washed and wrapped in a towel, I sit in front of Danielle and stare at the mirror. I have the usual anticipation of daydreaming about how it will look. I love change, and getting my hair cut is a quick, painless, and substantial change. Danielle leans back a bit, part stretch, part habit, as she takes off the towel and appraises the job ahead. Expertly and without hesitation, she selects a comb, and soon enough I look like Jedward with crocodile clips.

Now the serious business begins. Danielle pulls up a stool on wheels, plops down on it and, holding the scissors and comb with her right hand, she combs with the right, smooths with the left, passes the comb to the left hand and cuts with the right. Tilting her head to get a different view, she briefly pauses before continuing with the speed and confidence of Edward Scissorhands.

"Looking pretty thin these days," she comments. I say nothing in response, and thankfully, she moves to another subject without a break. Before long, she impatiently sits up and gets rid of the stool. Comb, smooth, cut, starting from the back, she works her way to the crown, not missing a beat despite the constant distractions. It's nothing short of poetry in motion.

Not just a hairdresser anymore, she has transformed in front of my eyes into a dedicated businesswoman, a true professional at work. Future mum, unflappable, charming, and engaging. She beams at me in the mirror.

"Not much longer now. Are you okay for time?" I feel the sun shining on me, a warm glow of genuine attention. I look back at the woman with the huge baby bump who has time for me, her husband who called because he lost his Oyster card, her client who needs reassurance, and the delivery boy who walked in looking for Derrick.

I wonder if she worries about her baby weight. Perhaps when you're married and pregnant, weight doesn't matter so much anymore, and you can relax and eat without feeling guilty. I luxuriate at the thought. Maybe someday weight won't matter so much. I glance at the mirror and almost fail to recognize the skinny girl with the fashionable bob who looks back at me. She has really done wonders with my limp and lifeless hair. I want to kiss her!

"Don't worry about me. I have all the time in the world," I respond, smiling back at her.

And I do.

Chapter Thirty-Three

Shopping

To motivate me to eat, Mom promised she would take us shopping at Lowery's Mall when I reached 48 kilos. Needless to say, a new dress two sizes too big would not be a good reason to become fat or give me any motivation whatsoever. I timed it carefully. A week before my period, when I was at my heaviest, wearing my heaviest and loosest outfit, I filled my inner pockets with Ella's juggling sand-filled squares, drank a litre of water, jumped on the scales, and called out to Mom. She ran up the stairs and hopefully looked at the scales, which showed just over 48 kilos.

"Take off your shoes," she instructed.

I knew she would do that, but I wasn't worried since I had already anticipated that. She smiled ear-to-ear and my heart went out to her. Wrong as she may be, I love my mom and want her to be happy more than anything else. A shopping trip is great but seeing her happy is even better.

The three of us piled in the car and headed for the mall. Most of my friends prefer shopping with their friends. I love going shopping with Mom and Ella. We usually go three times a year and it's always a fantastic day out. Lowery's Mall is laid out as a giant two-story cross, and we make sure we visit every single shop, starting with H&M, which is the closest shop to the car park.

Even before the lift door opens, Ella and I are jumping with anticipation and chattering on about all the possible ways we can spend the budget Mom has given us. We both know if we try something Mom really likes, she'll exceed the budget without hesitation. Usually I'm the one who goes over. Most times Ella ends up with extra money in her ever-swelling bank account.

Mom always ends up with a new pair of shoes to add to her growing collection. She loves shoes because, as she says, they never make her look fat. She has the daintiest size-four feet, and lucky Ella, who is also a size four, will inherit all the shoes, including Mom's prized Jimmy Choo's.

My watch says we have six hours to cover all of Lowery's, with a quick stop for refreshments. I don't think Mom can stand the full-day experience without her mid-shop white wine. As for Ella, she is happy with anything sugary. Krispy Crème is her snack of choice.

Walking in and out of shops with Mom and Ella, trying on shoes, earrings, dresses and tops, makes my heart swell. It's not all the new stuff which makes me happy. It's mostly a warm feeling of being safe and looked after by the two people in the world who love me the most, completely and unconditionally. I am a young kid again, and it feels like a heavy weight has been lifted off my shoulders. So much so that I agree to have a lollipop from the checkout girl at Mango's. It tastes divine, and for the first time in weeks, I'm not wondering about the calories.

Mom's credit card is getting a proper workout, but she doesn't seem to mind at all. She's also beaming for the first time in months. For a few hours we are all transported into an alternate universe where Dad is not being weird, I am not a slave to the scales, and both Ella and I can be carefree kids again. It's a feeling which makes my bottom lip quiver. I *so* want this feeling to last forever.

We are buying silly things. Fluffy socks, cheap earrings, hairclips, flip-flops. I can tell Mom is caught up in the same feeling and we just don't want it to end. We are laughing, trying on ridiculous things and not even once looking at our iPhones. We are inside a bubble of love, a moment in time which caught us by surprise. Then suddenly it is 6 p.m.

Our excursion is over.

Chapter Thirty-Four

Hungry

For the last three weeks or so I've only eaten roughly 3,000 calories and I am exercising loads. I have an essay due tomorrow morning which I have to finish tonight, but I'm so hungry I can't concentrate properly. I rushed through the essay so I could eat and sent it in without proofreading it. As soon as I hit send, I realized I had forgotten to put my name and the date on the cover sheet.

I rushed downstairs and took a banana from the fruit bowl. I ate it in two bites as I rummaged through the fridge. I ate two kilos of fruit and vegetables just sitting in front of the fridge. I don't think I chewed any of it. I felt terrible and threw it all up in a Tupperware bowl.

But I didn't stop there. I ate a can of tuna, a bag of nuts, a yogurt with lots of sugar, an avocado, and a bagel. In my haste, I bit the inside of my cheek and my tongue. I reached for the Tupperware and threw up again.

Then I went out in the dark for a run, did loads of squats, crunches, and jumping jacks to burn any lingering calories.

And yet after all this I am still so hungry! I am crying as I write this while at the same time writing an email to my teacher about forgetting to put my name on my homework. I'm doing all this standing up because it burns more calories. It's past midnight and I still have to get up early tomorrow and do my morning run.

This really sucks!

Chapter Thirty-Five

A Helping Hand

I like to stay on top of any new pills that come on the market which can help me stay on track with my diet. I've tried everything they have at Boots multiple times, but I don't think they're strong enough to make any difference. I found out about a new drug which stops your body from absorbing fat, but the pharmacist took one look and refused to sell it to me on the grounds that I was already too thin. I begged Ella to get it for me, as I was sure she qualifies, but he wouldn't give it to her, either.

Luckily, there is the Internet, where everything is available. Not only did I find the new pills, but I also found many other diet pills which are only available online. I ordered some of everything! My secret stash of drugs has grown impressively. I mostly use what I think is right for the occasion, but sometimes I take a little of everything, depending on how bad I've been with eating. I have diet pills, diuretics, laxatives, and caffeine pills, although these last ones don't work on me anymore.

I try to combine them, but sometimes I get it wrong and have terrible headaches or stomach aches. I take paracetamol for those and it helps a lot. I'm not sure how many pills I take each week, but it must be over thirty. I know when I've taken too many because I get this thumping on my chest like a giant drum. It's happened a couple of times and scared me. I want to be thin, not sick (or dead).

Today, I came up with an idea for sticking to my diet and also making Mom less worried about what I eat. I still eat the same amount of food, but I make it look like it's a lot more by cutting it into tiny pieces or very thin slices. Take a quarter of a chicken breast, for example. It doesn't look like a lot of food. Now, if you cut it up into many different pieces, you can fill a whole plate.

And here is the best part. You can eat less! It takes much longer to chew each piece, so you have more time to feel full, and Mom thinks I am eating more. Win-win! I can use the same trick for everything. Here is what my dinner looks like:

¼ chicken breast cut into small pieces
½ boiled egg cut up (this looks a bit messy)
¼ cucumber, thinly sliced
1 rice cake
1/3 cup zero-fat yogurt

This is 155 calories and a plateful of food. Assuming I have an apple and twenty grams of cornflakes for lunch, for another 120 calories, then I'll have eaten a lot of food for a total of 275 calories. With the apple, I'll cut it into really small pieces which last a long time. As for the cornflakes, they last until dinner if I eat them one at a time. If I want something sweet, I'll have sugar-free gum or a Diet Coke. It works well. I'm not hungry and Mom is not suspicious.

I can burn 300 calories easily, even just walking around school and doing crunches at home. If I slip and eat more, then I'll ask the coach driver to drop me off a few stops from home and I'll walk the rest of the way. To make the walk more efficient, I carry extra books in my backpack. The extra weight helps burn more calories.

Again, a win-win!

Chapter Thirty-Six

Don't Order Meds on the Internet

I have been throwing up regularly for over six months and something inside of me is beginning to tell me it may not be very good for me. I did a bit of research online, only to find out there are girls out there who have been purging for decades without experiencing any problems. I know I have a problem though. I have become so desensitized that I have to use the bristly side of the toothbrush to scrape my throat so I can gag. It's becoming so hard to throw up that I'm becoming desperate in my attempts.

I belong to a *thinspiration* group online, and I asked them about this problem. Thinspiration is full of inspirational photographs of beautifully-toned, super-thin girls. It's also a place to ask for advice on some of the more difficult questions about becoming and staying thin. It turns out my problem is quite common, and there is actually a good solution called Ipecac Syrup. It is illegal in this country, but it's very easy to get on the Internet. I used almost all my monthly allowance and ordered three bottles. I had to ship it to Ginny's house, as I'm sure that if Mom had seen a package

147

with foreign stamps on it, she would have asked me endless questions about it.

When it finally arrived, I couldn't wait to try it. The time came soon enough, as I had been binging on a regular basis. I didn't know what to expect, so I didn't want to try it at home. I decided to go to the park near our house. I brought a magazine to pass the time and chose a bench as far from the path as possible. It took thirty minutes for the medicine to work, and when it did, I effortlessly rid myself of everything I had eaten.

What I didn't know was the syrup would continue to work for another hour. The retching was so violent that I couldn't breathe. I felt very dizzy, and while I was still retching, I passed out on the grass behind a bush. I woke up hours later with a splitting headache and my heart racing furiously. I was shaking and my throat felt as if I had swallowed glass. My face was covered in half-digested food and I felt sick and disgusting. I stumbled to the nearest Starbucks and begged to use their bathroom. I cleaned myself off as best as I could and then ordered a smoothie, which I NEVER do, but I was so dehydrated. My heart was beating very strangely, and I was afraid I had done some serious damage.

Eventually, I felt well enough to walk home. On the way, I threw out the almost-full bottle of syrup. Lesson learned. I was going back to the toothbrush.

At least it won't kill me!

WINTER

Chapter Thirty-Seven

Dad Gets Beaten Up in the Park

The days have got super short, and by 4 p.m. it is pitch black. There is a short stretch of road through the park which we have to cross to get home. It is, of course, all up hill, dark and scary. Ella and I, with our phones hidden in our pockets, hold each other's hand and we run through it together. Mom says we are being ridiculous, but something happened that changed everyone's mind.

A few weeks before Christmas, our doorbell rang and then kept ringing until Mom got to the door. Standing at the doorstep was Dad, with a gash on his forehead, and two guys in uniform holding him up on either side. As it turned out, Dad had been walking through the same road looking at his iPhone, when a gang jumped him from behind. They stole his phone, his iPad, his computer, and his expensive watch which was a present from Mom. They savagely beat him up, kicked him on the head, and ran off. As he lay bleeding on the path, one of the attackers actually ran back and kicked him some more for no reason whatsoever.

We could all see Dad was shaken but trying to be brave about it. Quivering, Mom grabbed her keys and coat and— holding Dad—went out the door on the way to the hospital before the two detectives at the door had time to finish their story.

We heard the rest from Mom over breakfast. In the end, Dad only needed a few stitches, but he didn't look like himself as he sipped his coffee and scrolled through his messages. He told Mom that while it was happening, he was not in pain or afraid, almost as if it was happening to someone else, and he was just an observer.

Mom was distraught. She got on the phone to the school first thing in the morning and convinced them to change the route of our coach so we could be dropped off in front of our door. Mom can be unstoppable sometimes, and on this occasion both Ella and I were glad. After what had happened, I don't think I could have convinced Ella to go through that park in the dark ever again.

Dad's stiches were soon taken out, but he had changed in a way I couldn't explain. I heard Mamgu Winny tell Mom she thought that her son's head had been shaken so much that it had changed his personality. I could tell Mamgu Winny was worried. Her whole universe was our family. She wanted to spend the rest of her days surrounded by her son and grandchildren. Dad's weird personality changes unsettled her.

In our house, Mom was the one who made everything happen, and Mamgu Winny was happy that way. Dad was like a shadow of himself. He looked the same, but somehow, he was different. Ella and I, who normally jumped on his lap and cover him in kisses, suddenly felt shy, as if he was a stranger.

He was withdrawing from us.

Chapter Thirty-Eight

Christmas

The giant tree is up and all the baubles I have known since I was a baby are twinkling reassuringly. Mom, who loves Christmas, has been wrapping presents since early December, and the steadily-growing mountain of presents was making us giddy with anticipation. Not all was well, however. Mom and Dad appeared to be avoiding each other and Mamgu Winny tried hard to stay out of their way and keep us kids out of the way too. Dad's trips are getting longer and his phone buzzes a lot with calls which he always takes in another room or the garage. If I didn't know any better, I would have thought Dad was having an affair. I feel disloyal even thinking that and I'm sure it's not possible.

Dad and Mom are the closest couple amongst all the parents I know. They deeply love and care for each other and I cannot imagine either one of them would do anything to risk our family. Dad will be fifty this year and Mom keeps talking about how this is a difficult age and many men have a midlife crisis. When I talked to her about Dad the other day, she explained that we just need to wait for this to pass and it's nothing to worry about. Ella doesn't want to talk about it and shuts me down whenever I bring up Dad's weird behaviour. She's always been a Daddy's girl, and I think this whole thing is making her more upset than she lets on.

I hope I get cash for Christmas this year. Unless Mom comes up with an idea I have not thought about already, I'd rather buy my own presents. I suppose this is very unchristmassy, but my allowance is never enough for me to buy the things I want. I have also been hinting about the leather jacket I saw on ASOS. But it's £250. I doubt I'll be getting that! A slim, envelope-like package has appeared under the tree, so I may get cash after all.

Christmas morning is the best! Even though I said I wanted cash, I'm now thinking I'd rather have lots of packages to open. Mom puts so much effort into finding just the right presents for us, and watching her face light up as we open them makes me wish every day was Christmas morning.

I got £50 cash after all, but I also got a beauty box subscription and a fake leather jacket. What an amazing day. I am so happy! Ella also got a beauty box subscription and loads of clothes. Mom wanted to buy a replacement watch for Dad, but he told her not to get him one, so she got him a beautiful leather briefcase.

Dad asked us to get something for Mom for £200, so we got her perfume, a pair of earrings, and a cashmere scarf. She thanked him, but as she opened each present, she beamed at Ella and me. Nobody can fool Mom. She knew we had got her the presents.

Christmas brunch is always huge, and I've been obsessing about it for days. I've been binging on cookies and other stuff for weeks. It seems food is everywhere during Christmas. I've managed to get rid of almost all of it in one way or another and I am now 41 kilos. All the retching has made me feel a bit faint, but it passes really quickly.

Christmas brunch, however, is a whole different story. Everything I love is on the table and the whole family sits around it for what seems like hours. I love eggs benedict, and Mom has gone out of her way to make some for me. Dad ate quickly and left the table to disappear into his tablet. I can tell Mom is upset. She worked so hard to make everything perfect and off he goes. I'm mad at him for not showing any appreciation for her. I want to make Mom happy.

She puts the eggs in front of me and I start slowly picking around the edges of the toast, wondering about the calories and grams of fat I'll have to work off. Then I nick the egg, and a beautiful cascade of golden yolk covers the toast and mixes with the sauce. I wolf down the lot and tear through everything else on the table. Muffins, bagels, salmon, strawberries, chocolate cake, and lots of coffee. My stomach suddenly lurches, and I run for the loo. I hadn't eaten properly in a week and my body can't cope. I see it all coming back up, and I have a searing pain across my belly. When the spasms stop, I wipe my face and turn around. The whole family is standing by the door looking shocked. I can't help but notice Dad is not there.

Well done, Winny. I'd just ruined Christmas for everyone! I feel absolutely terrible. Looking at their worried faces, I realize how much they love me and my eyes well up with tears. Ella is holding a half-eaten muffin, probably wondering if she should put it down or finish it off. I sit up and force a big smile.

"I feel great now. Please don't worry. I just ate too fast and I have a bit of a stomach bug, I think. Let's go finish our breakfast." To make my point about feeling better, I grab the half-eaten muffin out of Ella's hand and take a big bite. "See, all good now," I say, but they don't look convinced.

I did ruin Christmas, after all.

Chapter Thirty-Nine

New Year

New year, new me.

My resolutions are many. For starters, I want to stop smoking, because it's bad for me and it's making me dizzy. I'll convince Ginny to do it with me. I also want to stop purging. Purging isn't an emergency lifesaver. All it does is give me a license to binge. My new goal will be to fast if I binge. This way, I will probably think twice before binging. Also, I want to stabilize my weight at just under 40 kilos. I could lose a bit more, but I can see that it's making Mom really upset and I don't want to give her any more things to worry about.

I'm also thinking about doing the ABC Diet for a week. I heard about it from one of the girls at school. She's probably the skinniest girl in the whole school, so I'm guessing it must work. What I like about it is that you start at 200 calories on Monday, but then it builds up all the way to 500 calories by Thursday, before you fast on Friday, and then eat 800 calories on Saturday and Sunday. This is great on so many levels. I can eat lots of food on the weekend when Mom is around and then during the week, I can use all my calories for dinner and eat nothing the rest of the day. I should call it the "Keep Mom Happy" diet.

For New Year's, I made a list of all the reasons I want to lose weight. I wrote everything in my journal so I can refer to it every time I feel really hungry. Here's the funny thing— the one food I find hard to resist are the bananas in the fruit bowl. Mom knows that and she always keeps it full. I simply can't spare the 100 calories, no matter how much I like them. Anyway, here is my list:

When I reach 40 kilos:

My dresses will hang off of me instead of hugging me.
I will be the tall girl without being the "big" girl.
I will be able to bend over in a swimsuit without my stomach touching itself.
I will not have gross fat hanging off my thighs.
I will not have that weird armpit fat.
I will be in the "underweight" category when I google my weight and height.
My ribs will show when I raise my hands above my head.
I will be able to see the outline of my rib cage when I wear a tube-top.
I will be the skinniest person in my friend group.
I will get those "wow, you're so skinny" comments.
I will be able to go to a restaurant and not have a "food baby" afterwards.
My waist will be beautiful in tight clothes.
I will be able to sit down and not have my thighs touch.

I will be able to slide bracelets on and off my wrist without undoing the clasp.
My friends will be asking me how I stay so skinny.
I will be able to wear anything and look great.

I plan to add to this as I think of other reasons, so I left a blank page next to the list.

I am generally feeling positive and energetic. The only sad thing in my life right now is that Mom and Dad are the worst I have ever seen them with each other. Whenever Mom asks him something, all he says is, "Whatever," and then he withdraws and becomes silent. He had a week off work, and he spent most of it in the basement working out. We can hear him grunting, and the banging of the weights as he drops them on the floor vibrates throughout the house. He comes up at mealtimes, but then he showers and leaves the house, sometimes not returning until very late. He says he has work to do at the office. Mom stays up reading, waiting for him, but sometimes he sleeps in the guest room, supposedly so as not to wake us up.

I've found a new way to not think of food all the time. It's neither good nor bad. When I fast all day, around 4 p.m. I start getting very hungry—like, *really* hungry. I discovered that if I have a large glass of diet tonic water followed by a glass of wine, I forget about food and get really buzzy and creative. With the holidays, there have been many open bottles of wine, so nobody notices anything missing. I will also try vodka or even whiskey instead of wine to see if they have the same effect. Our liquor cabinet has many dusty, half-finished bottles of forgotten alcohol which nobody will miss. The total calories are twenty for the gin and 110 for the wine, which is significant, I grant you, but the feeling is great.

I'd rather spend my calories this way.

Chapter Forty

January

School started yesterday and I'm determined to catch up with all my missing homework and do better. Physics is too far gone, and I don't think it's possible to catch up anymore, so I asked Mom to write to the headmistress and ask her to let me drop it. After all, she had warned me against taking four difficult subjects. Now I feel much better and can concentrate on the other three. Getting any A's is probably beyond my grasp at this stage, but I have my heart set on getting at least three B's. It will take lots of work, but I can do it, I know it.

I started the year by clearing my desk of all the bits and bobs that had found their way onto a pile next to my Mac. Most of it I threw out, but some of the best memes I had printed I kept, as I wanted to show Ginny—if she ever speaks to me again. She's been really cold with me recently and avoids me at school. I can understand that she probably feels jealous.

For the first time since nursery school, I am thinner than her. I now have a graceful collarbone which can be seen clearly, even under my jumper. As for my hips, I am so skinny you can easily feel the bones. I know this sounds like I'm skin and bones, but this is really not the case. I have plenty of fat on my sides and above my knees. Thankfully, until I lose it for good, I can hide it with the right cut of trousers.

This term, they started offering yoga after school and I signed up right away. I read that it's really good for your flexibility and your state of mind. And I think I really need it. My mind has been all over the place, and I can think of little else other than what I'm going to eat next and when. I started a food diary where I write down all the food I plan to eat every day and the number of calories in each food. I try to stay between 300 and 500 calories by filling up on foods which have very few calories. Celery, tomatoes, strawberries, lettuce, and cabbage are some of my staples. I have been drinking loads of diet soda, coffee, and tea because it makes me less hungry.

Unfortunately, it also makes me jittery and puts me in a crappy mood. The tonic water and wine idea works much better, and I've been working my way through the liquor cabinet. I had a screaming fight with Ella over dinner because she put oil on the salad before I had a chance to fill my plate. Afterwards, she looked really hurt and I felt super bad, but it was too late to take it back.

I went to the first yoga class after school. It turns out I needed two mats because I am too skinny. It made me feel terrific, despite the pain and the bruises that showed up the next day along my spine and on my hips. I'm finally one of those girls who needs special treatment because of my thinness.

Kind of like a model. Smashing!

Chapter Forty-One

A New Beginning

Last night I had a dream. I was wearing a white nighty from when I was little, and my pink and yellow unicorn slippers. I walked to the large mirror we have in our living room and then effortlessly took a little step and walked right into it.

The funny thing was, I wasn't at all afraid. I felt incredibly good, safe, and healthy. I wandered around our living room and up the stairs to Mom and Dad's bedroom. I saw them sleeping, facing each other, their heads almost touching.

I walked into Ella's room. She was snoring in the bottom bunk of our old bunk bed from when we used to share a room. I glided past her and looked at her open diary. A million hearts jumped out and I found myself in a cloud of hearts. A warm glow surrounded me as I jumped out of the mirror in the hallway and I was back in our real house.

This morning I woke up feeling the best I have felt for months. I was full of happy energy. I dressed extra nice for school and put a bit of fake tan on my face under my makeup. Today I was going to shine at school and be friendly and sociable. I would ask questions in class and I would invite Ginny and Megan to come over to my house for a sleepover this coming weekend. Suddenly, I realized that there was nothing I wanted more than to get my friends back and to do things together. I played happy music on the way to school and felt really great.

School was also wonderful. I could see that my teachers were delighted to have the old Winny back, and when I handed in the homework I'd completed on the coach journey, Ms. Hinchcliff, our form tutor, looked as if she wanted to hug me.

Had I really been all that bad? I couldn't tell for sure, but judging by everyone's reaction, I must have been. At lunch, I piled my plate high with salad and two hard-boiled eggs, and I also took a small pack of raisins and a banana. I pushed aside any thoughts of restraint and luxuriated in my eating extravaganza. I sat next to my friends, who hadn't seen me in the dining hall since the beginning of the year. They appeared stunned but were also very welcoming. We chatted like old times, as if the past several months of coolness and isolation had never happened. Was it really that easy to repair bridges? Both Ginny and Megan agreed to come over Friday after school for a sleepover, and to my astonishment, Hannah and Lila said that they were free as well. Woo-hoo!

My excellent mood continued all day. When Mom glanced at me hopefully during dinner, I smiled and passed my plate to her.

"I will have breast," I said, pointing at the roasted chicken, "and some salad. No potatoes, please." She didn't push her luck and I cleared my plate. With lunch, I figured I had eaten a total of 900 calories—900 calories that made everybody happy. It was a small price to pay.

That night, with my belly full, I slept like a baby.

Chapter Forty-Two

Thin

This morning, the scale showed 40 kilos. I am officially the thinnest I have ever been. I only need to lose three more kilos and I will stop for good. I'm looking pretty decent even at this weight and I can wear anything I want, but I mostly wear baggy clothes to avoid criticism and strange looks at school.

I must have lost all my body fat, which is good, but I'm always freezing. I can't wait for winter to be over. I never noticed it before, but my hands are always a weird blue and grey colour, probably from the low temperatures. Gloves help a lot. I have a very nice pair from Accessorize that I wear almost all the time, even indoors. On the bright side, I've not had a period in months. Who wants the hassle of that, anyway?

Ella told me I look disgusting, that I'd be prettier if I gained weight. That right now, I look like a corpse. I really wish she wasn't this jealous. It must be hard to be her, with all of her rolls and dimples. Nothing really fits her or looks good on her. She has zero willpower, and even though I tried to help her with the toothbrush trick, she told me it was disgusting, and she was going to tell Mom on me. I told her I was just kidding. Mom has been off my back lately dealing with her problems and I don't want her dragging me to therapy again.

"You are very, *very* thin," Ella mumbled, having lost her earlier bravado.

"Thank you," I said defiantly.

She looked so shocked and flustered, almost tearful, and then hastened to clarify.

"That wasn't a compliment! You don't look good!"

"I don't care if I look good. I care if I look thin, so back off, fatty!"

In her usual Ella way, she promptly burst into tears. What a loser—and not the good kind. I wish she would listen to me and lose some weight.

She'd be so much happier.

Chapter Forty-Three

A Sleepover

Since everyone agreed to come over to mine for a sleepover, I had been driving Mom crazy with instructions and questions.

Should we eat at the table or in my bedroom? What should we eat? Could we have one beer each? Would Mom take Ella to the movies and get her out of the house? Could I borrow her wireless speaker? What should I wear? Could we borrow her curling iron? Could Dad bring the sleeping bags from the garage?

Mom was so happy that my friends were coming over that she agreed to everything and even gave me extra pocket money for Victoria Secret PJs. We went to the mall together after school that Thursday. I chose a pair of silk pyjamas and they gave me a free pair of slippers. Mom encouraged me to try on a new bra as well, and I was surprised that she didn't bat an eyelid about the price.

The only thing that marred the afternoon was when I caught her staring at me in the mirror through the gap in the curtain of the changing room. She looked sad, as if her previous smiling face was a mask she had taken off when she glimpsed me. I didn't know what to make of it. I looked at my reflection critically. The light was horrible, but my belly was flat and there was a lovely gap between my thighs. I thought I looked alright, especially considering I'd been steadily eating 800 to 1,000 calories every day.

Friday finally arrived, and I managed to shoo everyone out of the house. Mamgu Winny promised to stay in her flat, and Dad was nowhere to be seen. Probably off on some business function. Ella and Mom went to see *Inside Out* and assured me they would stay out until 11 p.m.

We girls had a blast. I made popcorn. I only had five kernels. We had pizza and I picked off the cheese, but then ate it anyway. Then we all squeezed onto my bed sucking on our strawberry laces and chatting away. Every now and then we would share a ciggie, hanging as far out of the window as possible. It was magical, and it felt as if a giant weight had been taken off my shoulders. They poked at my hip bones and slid the entire pizza box between the gap in my thighs to show me how skinny I was. We all collapsed on the floor laughing, with the pizza box still wedged between my knees.

All of the awkwardness of the past few months evaporated like mist in the sunshine, and we each had more than the one beer Mom said we could have. We even used the house phone to call all the boys we liked and quickly hung up before they recognized any of our screeching voices. We carried on like that until Mom and Ella peeked through my bedroom door to let us know they were back.

"Have you girls been smoking?" she asked. We all vigorously denied it, and very unusually for her, Mom accepted our answer and walked out, dragging Ella along with her, without pressing for more answers. I could hear Ella through the door begging to be allowed to join our group, but soon their voices faded away.

We stayed up all night, and only when the sky started turning grey did we fall asleep. I went to close the curtains against the morning light, and I saw Dad in his business suit walking up to the front door. My last thought was for Mom.

Her heart must be breaking.

Chapter Forty-Four

A Very Bad Day

I am the sort of person who trusts everyone and believes in the goodness of people. Yesterday, I was proven wrong. I now feel dirty and disgusting. Mark, who I have secretly loved for ages, finally paid me some attention.

During break, halfway through maths tutoring, he asked me out. I was so happy! I spent hours deciding what to wear, carefully applying my barely-visible makeup and the new push up bra I bought after saving my allowance like *forever*. I quickly checked on YouTube how to hide the dark circles under my eyes. I've not been sleeping well and it's beginning to show. I'm not hungry anymore during the night, but I wake up with my heart racing and then I can't go back to sleep.

It felt really good to pull up my new black mini skirt, a full size smaller than a month ago. It hung beautifully on my hips.

When I met Mark, he said we should go hang out at his best friend's house whose parents were away. This made me a bit nervous, but I agreed to go anyway. When we arrived, we found two of Mark's friends in the living room drinking beer. Mark joined them, but I decided to skip on the calories. I don't like beer, anyway. Mark's friend came back from the living room with a bottle of vodka and I had a few shots of that to build up my confidence.

After we had a few drinks, Mark said we should go find one of the other rooms for more privacy. This made me uncomfortable, but I didn't know how to back out without looking foolish. I wasn't sure if I wanted to have sex with him on our first date, and what if he wanted me to do stuff I found gross?

As soon as the door closed behind us, he pushed me on the bed and started tugging at my clothes. I tried to push him off, but he was too strong. Ignoring my whimpering, he pulled off my skirt, turned me over and pushed my head into the pillow. This muffled my cries as I started struggling to breathe. He wrestled, trying to push his way in, but he couldn't manage it.

Then it got much, much worse. I heard him calling out to his friends.

"Come hold down the skinny bitch."

The door burst open, and I thought if I didn't suffocate, I would die from embarrassment. They were rough. One actually sat on me, pushing me down. It hurt so much, but I could only whimper while trying not to choke. I closed my eyes and tried to transport myself to a safe place far away, hoping it would end soon.

When they were finished, they told me to leave and warned me to keep my mouth shut.

"Who's gonna believe you? You came looking for it."

I sobbed quietly as I pulled up my skirt, leaving behind my ripped tights. I staggered home, managing to avoid Mom and Ella, who were chattering in the kitchen.

I wasn't going to say anything about what had just happened, of course. The embarrassment was too much to bear. I remembered their words and threats. Had I been looking for it? What was I expecting? I had a very long shower, and then ate my entire secret stash of candy crisps and nuts. Immediately afterwards, I went to the bathroom and purged.

Right then and there, I decided that I was done with boyfriends. I would concentrate on myself and my schoolwork from now on, but I was done with maths tutoring. I would never go back there. I felt dirty and disgusting and I could never face Mark or his friends again. I would have to find a good excuse for dropping tutoring right before exams.

I'm not sure how other girls find the courage to go to the police when this happens to them. I just want to forget it ever happened. I would never tell a soul, not even Ginny. After all, they didn't really hurt me, and they'd probably say I deserved it. I did have a date with Mark, after all, and I was also drunk, and I had worn my super short black skirt. What did I think was going to happen? That we would play Monopoly?

My final thought before I fell asleep was that there was a bright side. I decided to ignore that he'd called me a bitch and concentrate on the positive, like they said to do in group therapy.

Mark called me skinny.

Chapter Forty-Five

Please—No More Restaurants and Dinner Parties

Considering how tight the money situation is, I'm amazed by how often Mom decides we should all go out to dinner. Does she think I will eat more if we do? I always order a salad without dressing, and it's torture to watch others tuck into Chinese or pizza for hours on end. Most times, I say I have too much homework and I stay at home and exercise.

Mom always brings back an extra portion for me, and I feel really guilty when I flush it down the toilet or hide it in the back of my closet. Funny story—I forgot that I had hidden a box of pizza under my bed, and when I fell asleep, I kept dreaming I was at Pizza Hut stuffing my face. It was more of a nightmare, actually...

Dinner parties are even worse, because Mom insists that I go, even when I have homework for real. The last one was a bit of a disaster. After taking one bite of the lasagna, I put my napkin on the plate to make it impossible to eat more.

Mom's best friend Emily, who had lovingly cooked for hours, looked aghast, and everyone stopped eating and were staring at me, appalled. I got up and took the offending plate to the kitchen. I tried to rinse the linen napkin under cold water, but the tomato stain would not come off.

Then I did something I am completely not proud of. Standing next to the sink, I literally inhaled the rest of the lasagna without even chewing it. I even walked to the bin to throw it out, but then I just kept eating. The pan was in the sink and I could see bits of cheese stuck to the sides. I took a knife and scraped them off and then ate them too.

And this is what happens when I am forced to sit in front of food when I'm really hungry! I was angry at myself, but I was also angry at everyone else as well. I couldn't even go to the bathroom, because it was right next to the dining room and someone would probably hear me purge.

I went for a run the moment we got home!

Chapter Forty-Six

What is Wrong with Me?

Mom stopped my daily runs. She says that unless I put on some weight and start eating properly, exercise can be dangerous for my health. She also wrote a note to the school, asking them to excuse me from PE. This is a bit ridiculous I think, especially since exercise is very good for your health. I tried to go out running at 5 a.m. the other day and found Mom dozing on the sofa at the bottom of the stairs. She heard me coming down and waved me back upstairs without a word.

I've been getting up at night to secretly and quietly do my crunches. I really don't want to end up looking flabby. And because of lack of exercise, I've been sleeping very poorly. I find that I sleep better after my 1,000 crunches, but on the other hand, they leave me with this strange feeling where my heart races for several minutes before it goes back to normal. It may be because I'm doing them so quickly, as I always worry that someone will walk in on me and I'll be found out. It's quite ridiculous that I have to exercise in secret, but Mom is adamant.

I went to the chemist yesterday and bought a hair-strengthening shampoo. My hair is looking much thinner these days, and I've noticed that when I use conditioner, quite a bit of my hair ends up in the drain. I don't want to end up bald at seventeen!

I've tried to speak to Mom about all this, but her only response is that I'm missing this and that nutrient in my diet and this is why my hair is falling out. She just wants me to be fat and I want to stay thin and this is the long and short of it. Mom can sure be infuriating sometimes. My hair and my weight are two separate things.

Why does she have to use everything to make a point when there is no point to be made?

Chapter Forty-Seven

I Hate School

This year is the hardest ever and I have lost interest in all the subjects I chose at the beginning of the year. These exams will be brutal. I try hard to concentrate and finish my homework, but it feels like I have a woolen ball clogged in my head.

Like the opposite of sharp razor, my thinking is slow and tangled. We just got the results from our mocks and my results were terrible. I don't even have passing grades in Maths and Chemistry. Mom is upset with me, and even Dad took his head out of his iPad long enough to say how disappointed in me he is. To be honest, I don't really care about grades, but I don't want to disappoint my parents.

My teachers are nice, but recently they've been treating me as if I'm sick. They don't even seem to mind when I've not done my homework. I'm beginning to believe they have given up on me going to a good uni. They've pretty much said so during the parent-teacher meeting. I felt really bad for Mom and Dad, who have only got compliments about me in the past. I found all of this to be a bit depressing and I had

185

a good cry in the car after the meeting. I made a vow to myself and Mom that afternoon.

I will try harder.

Chapter Forty-Eight

Hungry

Today I asked Megan if she wanted to have lunch with me. When the bell rang, we went to the dining hall together and joined the queue. I stood in line behind her for twenty minutes, but when it was my turn, I just wasn't hungry anymore, so I left the queue and waited for her after the cashiers. After she paid, she gave me a dirty look, which was completely unnecessary.

What and when I eat is my business, and my business alone. I made up a story that I had forgotten my lunch card at home, but then she offered to share her lunch with me, so I had to come clean.

"I'm just not hungry," I told her before she launched into a full-blown tirade.

"How can you not be hungry? Look at you. You look like a skeleton! Your breath smells of vomit and you can't even finish a full sentence. I can't watch you do this to yourself anymore. Are you trying to starve yourself to death?"

She waited for me to say something, or to deny her accusations, but I felt too tired and dispirited to respond at all. All the good feelings from the sleepover had disappeared, and my friends were once again hostile and distant towards me. She turned around and went and sat with some other girls from class.

Still holding my empty tray, I felt really self-conscious and teary, so I set the tray down and headed for the toilets, hoping to score a ciggie. A few girls were there, and even though I didn't get a full one, one kind soul shared hers as she wiped my tears.

I fainted at school yesterday. I bent over to pick up my bag and the next thing I saw was Ginny's worried face as she cradled my head on her lap. My heart was beating like a drum and I was short of breath for a few minutes. Ginny was waving her hands and calling for help at the top of her lungs. I told her to stop the drama and got back on my feet. I was a bit unsteady, but I didn't want to wait for a teacher to come over, so I picked up my bag and ran home. I suspect Ginny will tell Ella or a teacher. She's not been very supportive recently. I think she's jealous because I'm now quite a bit thinner than she is. She's always trying to make me eat. I hate that.

I've been fasting for two days, which is probably why I felt dizzy at school. Nobody was home when I got there, but there was a divine smell coming from the kitchen counter. Mom had made brownies. I am disgusted with myself just thinking of what I did next.

Standing by the counter, I ate the whole pan of brownies, and then a whole loaf of bread, some cold potato soup from the fridge, and the leftover spaghetti from last night's dinner. There was only one thing I could do after all this binging. I found the Ipecac from under the corner of the carpet where

I'd hidden it and took four pills with a diet soda. In no time, I was retching violently and barely made it to the bathroom. I hadn't chewed anything, so it got stuck in my throat and I started choking. If I died this way, it would really be the most stupid and pathetic death ever. In the end, I had to pull the ball of spaghetti out of my throat using my fingers.

When Ella came home from school, she found me rolling on the bathroom floor crying, all messy and dirty. I was so weak and exhausted I couldn't even move, and my heart was racing as if I had just run a marathon under the sun. She cleaned me up as best as she could and helped carry me to bed. I fell asleep instantly, but not before making her promise she wouldn't tell anyone.

I slept soundly for the rest of the afternoon and felt so much better when I woke up. I stripped and headed to the scales to assess the damage—39.5 kilos!

Yep. Still fabulous.

Chapter Forty-Nine

Pro Ana—Finally, a Group Who Gets Me

My UWG (Ultimate Weight Goal) is 35 kilos. I joined a Pro Ana forum and it's packed with tips and ideas for losing weight. This is a group which outwardly promotes anorexia. I am not really anorexic, but I think being part of a community like this will be motivating and wonderful. I would love to become as thin as some of the girls in this group.

I have settled on a moderate diet of 300 calories a day and lots of exercise. Today I woke up at 2 a.m. and jogged in place for six hours. I want to get to 10,000 steps in one day. During chemistry class, I tried to keep it up by tapping my feet in place, until Mr. Soley came over to my desk and put an end to it.

My Pro Ana group is full of Rules (with a capital R). I get that. You need to set rules for yourself, and if you are truly dedicated, you will have no problem sticking to them. Rules are everything. Examples: Don't eat anything white. Do not, under any circumstances, eat after 6 p.m. Don't eat before 3 p.m. Cut each bite into X number of pieces. Chew X amount of times. Do not eat anything that has over three grams of fat, etc.

I got lots of great ideas from the group, like swirling food in your mouth without swallowing, which makes you feel as if you actually ate it. It actually works really well with chocolate and yogurt. Here is another one I will try:

Cut a ribbon the size you want your waist to be. Wrap and tie it around your wrist like a bracelet. Every time you look at it, you'll be reminded of your goals. When you're tempted, take it off and wrap it around your waist. See how close you are, or how far you have to go, and resist the temptation to eat.

Many of the girls on the forum like to spend time in supermarkets reading the calories on packaging. This, I don't get. Many have dropped out of school or are failing. I would never do this to Mom or to myself. I am defo going to uni.

I took a series of selfies, trying different angles to hide my fat bits, and created a signature with my starting weight, current weight, goal weight, and UWG (Ultimate Weight Goal). The older members of the group call UWG the scary one, but I'm not really scared. I feel truly excited, motivated, and empowered. It's great to have friends who share your passion, even if they're only virtual.

The members of the group have all sworn to follow the "Ten Commandments of Thinness." It's great to see them all written down in one place. I have been following all of them already without even realizing it. I copied them down in my diary. Here they are:

If you aren't thin, you aren't attractive.
Being thin is more important than being healthy.
You must buy clothes, cut your hair, take laxatives, starve yourself, and do anything to make yourself look skinnier.
You shall not eat without feeling guilty.
You shall not eat fattening food without punishing yourself afterwards.
You shall count calories and restrict intake accordingly.
What the scale says is the most important thing.
Losing weight is good and gaining weight is bad.
You can never be too thin.
Being thin and not eating are signs of true willpower and success.

These are my new Ten Commandments.

Chapter Fifty

My Thoughts Are Revealed

If you don't want something to be found, hide it well. This is the lesson I learned today. Mom found my diary and my world as I've known it came to an end. First of all, I can't believe she would do such a thing. Even if she had found my diary by mistake, it is *private*.

My private thoughts!

She should never have read it. Except she did. Cover to cover. I walked in from school and there it was on the kitchen counter. Mamgu Winny was there, and so was Mom. I could tell Mom had been crying. Her eyes were puffy, and she was doing that weird thing with her nose—a half sniffle, half snort.

"Ten Commandments?" she said.

And then she said the worst possible thing I could hear. "I feel so sorry for you. Sad, pitiful, and sick."

She went on to say I needed help, that she and Mamgu Winny would now be watching my every move and every single thing I eat, that she would tell the school to make sure I had lunch every day and *ate* it without sneaking off to the bathroom to purge. And of course, there would be a lot more therapy—privately, if necessary.

I just stood there half listening, while furiously thinking about how I could get out of this situation. Mom clearly didn't feel at all guilty that she had invaded my privacy, and she was not about to apologize. My life was about to become much, much harder to control. I tried to remember what I had written that was the most damaging. Clearly, the Ten Commandments had struck a chord. I'd also written my resolutions from the New Year, as well as my daily food intake.

Then there were some poems about love, friendship, and loneliness, and detailed descriptions of all the slights I had suffered from my friend group.

With nothing to say and feeling both embarrassed and angry at the same time, I chose to grab the offending diary off the counter and disappear into my bedroom.

If Mom wanted to make plans for spying on me, she would have to do it without my help, that's for sure.

Chapter Fifty-One

A Kind Doctor

Since the diary incident, my life has become hell. I have to go to the bathroom with the door open and I'm never allowed to close my bedroom door either. I am watched all the time. At school, I have to eat lunch next to the school nurse, who is not fooled by my carefully cut up lunch. She wants me to eat pizza, fish and chips, and mac and cheese. Gross, fatty stuff full of calories. She won't let me leave until I eat at least half of what she puts in front of me. It's pure torture for both of us.

I've been filling my pockets with chewed up food every time she looks at her phone. Talk about disgusting, but what else can I do?

I tried to do the same trick at home, but there are too many eyes watching, and Ella, supposedly *out of love*, has become an accomplished tell-tale spy. All of my privileges have been taken away from me and are handed back based on my daily weigh-in. I have to be weighed in my underwear, so there is no fooling Mom with extra weights in my pockets. I am so depressed, and I cry most of the time. Mom seems unmoved and determined.

My solution? I just stopped eating altogether. They can't physically force me to eat.

Dad's insurance agreed to pay for 24 sessions of private therapy, and when I stopped eating, it was arranged extremely quickly. The doctor took one look at me and suggested I be admitted to hospital, where they can stabilize my weight. But I absolutely refused. I am almost eighteen, and they can't make me. The compromise was that I have to see him three times a week after school. Mom comes with me and sits in the waiting room for the whole hour. Dad is just as worried, but he simply doesn't have the time off work.

I have to admit I'm liking all the attention and have taken an honest liking to my doctor. He is extremely attentive and listens to everything I say very carefully, only rarely interrupting with a question. He comes from a place of love. I can see that. He's been working with people who have eating disorders all his career and has even written a book on the subject. I told him during our first meeting that mine was not an eating disorder. I just wanted to be skinny. I didn't want to waste his time. But he said he didn't mind, and we could just talk, which was fine with me.

He told Mom she should give me some leeway. I explained to him how embarrassing it was to sit next to the nurse at school when I ate my lunches, and he convinced Mom that it was counterproductive. In the eight weeks the therapy lasted, I felt much relieved from all the stress which had been accumulating. I didn't gain any weight, but Mom was content that I didn't lose any, either.

I just bided my time. Nobody, not even my Mom, can keep up this sort of vigilance forever. I played along and waited to regain everyone's trust. It wasn't difficult. They all wanted me to get better, so when I started asking Mom to cook my favourite meals, they took it as a sign that I was ready to start eating again. At school, I'd use my Uniware card to buy a full meal. I wouldn't eat it, of course, but Mom would see it on her statement and assume I had. I felt a little guilty that I was wasting their money.

But they had left me no choice in the matter.

Chapter Fifty-Two

An Unexpected Visit

I missed two days of school this week. I felt too cold and too weak to get out of bed. Mom had gone to a meeting with the headmistress of Whiteheath to discuss what they were going to do with my schoolwork. Mamgu Winny had a hospital appointment, so I was left on my own for the first time in weeks.

When I went to the bathroom, I took the whole duvet with me, and still I was shivering. I think all my fat is gone. I am really happy about that, but I am also feeling as if I lack energy and have difficulty concentrating. I stayed in bed and watched Netflix for two days straight. I have tons of homework, but I can't bring myself to do it. I wrote a few posts in my Pro Ana group and got a few replies. Many of the girls said they were very cold even in the summer.

I stalked all my friends on Instagram. They look happy doing fun things. I haven't posted anything on Instagram in ages. I looked through my photos and posted one of my favourites. It's artistic, showing my back with my head turned slightly towards the lens. You can see the graceful curve of my back and my slight shoulders. My hair is all on one side, so it looks fuller than it is at the moment. I waited to see how many likes I would get.

An hour later I had only six likes, and two were from Ella and Rosie. It's lunch time at school, so everybody must have seen it! This is really depressing. Everyone must think I'm too ugly to even pretend to like. I looked at the tray Mom had left next to my bed before she went out. Spaghetti Bolognese piled high with cheese. I ate everything quickly and without chewing. The cake, too. Then I went downstairs and ate loads more, straight from the pot. I just stood there over the stove and stuffed my face. I was eating and crying, feeling terribly sorry for myself.

Nobody likes me. I am alone. I am a pathetic pig.

I collapsed on the floor, wrapped in my duvet, which was now covered in tomato splatters. I must have been howling, because the door burst open and Rosie's mum, Mrs. Johnson, ran in wearing her slippers and holding a pink curler. She took one look at me and started calling for an ambulance.

"I'm okay, Mrs. Johnson. It's just tomato sauce. I slipped and fell," I lied.

She put the phone down and came over to me.

"Sweetheart," she cooed, and wrapped her arms around me. "Here, here. Let me pick you up off this cold floor." She lifted me as if I was a feather and carried me to the sofa. She wiped my nose and my tears and liked my Instagram story.

"Nobody likes me. I am so ugly, boring, and fat," I wailed. She pulled out her phone and gave me another like.

Now I had nine likes and two *loves*. I felt a little better. Mrs. Johnson has a way about her that makes everyone feel safe. Since we were little girls, she baked cookies with Rosie and me, made plasticine princesses, and let us cover one wall of her house with finger paint.

"When did you lose all this weight?" she asked as she moved the duvet and peeked under it.

"I have been dieting for months," I demurred. "I still need to lose a couple of kilos, though."

"You don't want to lose all of your fat," she told me. "You will lose your boobies."

I burst out laughing. Boobies? Who calls breasts *boobies*?

Then I thought of Mom and Dad and a fresh wave of tears overcame me.

"I think Mom and Dad may get divorced. They argue all the time. I'm so scared our family will break up. I lost all my friends, and now this." I was crying so hard, I don't think she could fully understand all I was saying, but just being in her warm, comforting arms was making me feel better already.

Slowly, my sobs turned to hiccups and I started thinking I had to get away from her and try to get rid of all the spaghetti in my belly, which was beginning to feel as if I had swallowed a large rock. It would have to be a double effort of purging what I could and then exercise to get rid of the calories that for sure had been absorbed by now. I let her drone on about young girls being too thin these days as I calculated the calories of my stupid indulgence.

As I realized I must be well over 3,000 calories, I burst into a fresh wave of tears. Just thinking of the amount of exercise I would have to do made me extremely depressed and anxious. Over eight hours—when I was already feeling wiped out. If I could escape detection from Mom, then I could also fast for 24 hours. Then I would only need to do four hours exercise to stay at the same weight. I looked past Mrs. Johnson at the kitchen clock. It had only been an hour, which meant only about half of the calories would be in my system by now.

She was holding me tight and showed no sign of leaving. I regretted telling her about Mom and Dad. She couldn't do anything about it, anyway. Meanwhile, she seemed quite determined to stay right there on the sofa until Mom got home. I wiggled my way out of her arms and asked if she would make us a cup of tea while I had a shower. She fell for it. I was free.

Later that day, when Mom got home and found the empty plates by my bed and the substantial dent I had made on the leftovers in the pot, there was a serious lifting of the mood in the house. She kissed my wet hair and then made Mrs. Johnson a cup of coffee, and the two of them had a long chat over the kitchen table.

I turned on the TV in the living room and pretended not to hear what they were talking about, but of course I caught bits and pieces of the conversation. Mrs. Johnson got a fresh wave of Stokes' tears as Mom unloaded all her frustration and sadness from the past year. Soon they cracked open a bottle of wine and Mom shut the door. One thing was clear to me. Dad and I had made her life hell during the past year, and she had discovered something on Dad's computer which convinced her there was another woman.

Poor, poor Mom.

I ran upstairs and quietly started doing crunches. I counted all the way up to 875 before I heard the door open and close, and Mom's footsteps on the stairs. She wanted to make sure I hadn't heard any of the conversation, and that if I had, I was going to keep it to myself. She assured me I had nothing to worry about and Dad was just preoccupied because of a work problem. I looked at her puffy eyes and pretended to totally believe her. We sat on the bed desperately hugging. I felt her love like a warm blanket. I stayed unmoving, wishing I was still a little girl and time would not move.

I think she felt the same.

Chapter Fifty-Three

Hair

My beautiful red hair has been falling out in the shower for months. I've cut it twice, hoping to revive it, and have taken vitamins and biotin with no improvement. This morning I woke up and most of my hair was on my pillow like a halo. I jumped out of bed so quickly that I became really dizzy and had to sit back down for a minute to recover.

"My hair, my hair!" I cried out, so desperately that Mom heard me from downstairs and came running into my room. I could hear Mamgu Winny taking one creaky step at a time, trying to come to me as fast as her legs could carry her. Ella was the first to reach me and the horror on her face told me all I needed to know.

I was hysterical. In the bathroom mirror, I could see bald patches as big as a nickel all over my head. I didn't want to go back to my bed and lie with the remains of my hair, so I just collapsed on the bathroom floor sobbing and wailing. Every time someone tried to touch me, I'd let out a scream and a fresh wave of hysteria would overcome me. When I calmed down a bit, Mom agreed I didn't have to go to school and she would call Danielle and get me an appointment that morning.

She left my room to get her phone and I waved the other two out as well. I wanted to be alone to fully immerse myself in my misery. This was all my fault. It's no secret that restricted dieting plays havoc with the body. My muscles had disappeared, my periods were gone, I was cold as ice, my heart was beating funny, and now I had lost my hair—my trademark red mane was lying like a dead animal on my pillow. I was devastated. A little voice in my head kept reminding me that I deserved to look hideous. My outside matched my ugly inside. Depressed and full of black thoughts, I had never felt so low in my life. It was at that moment I truly saw what I had done to myself and my family. Losing my hair was really the nail in the coffin.

A fresh wave of tears overcame me. I had already lost everything—my friends, my college plans, my Mom's trust, my body, my health, my confidence, and my personality. But my hair was the final straw. Standing in front of the mirror, I decided enough was enough. I was going to change. I would ask to see a therapist and I would work hard at school.

Mom came back upstairs and told me Danielle would see me that afternoon. Almost shyly, she asked me if I wanted some breakfast. I nodded. *Yes*, I would. I had not eaten in 24 hours and suddenly I was ravenous. She left the room, taking with her the offending pillow with the remains of my hair.

Before I went downstairs, I made plans to see Ginny after my hair appointment. She was surprised to hear from me. I realized I hadn't called her in weeks, and she was supposed to be my best friend.

"Ginny, I lost all my hair." I sniffled and wiped my nose. "I've missed you so much. I've not been a good friend. I'm going to change," I promised. "Everything is going to change."

I jumped in the shower, got dressed and went down for breakfast.

It was the first morning in over a year that I left the bathroom without weighing myself.

Things were going to change for sure.

SPRING

Chapter Fifty-Four

As If I Am Not There

I sit at the kitchen table and pick up a fork. Lunchtime is always a funny time for me. Today I've been feeling hungry, so I'm looking forward to Mom's lunch call, but at the same time I've also been dreading it. I have to be strong and disciplined, choose what I eat carefully, chew slowly, and stop before I'm full. That's hard to do when I'm so hungry.

Mom, Dad, and Ella are already digging in. I quickly scan the spread and my stomach does a somersault. All of my favourites are there, and everything is very fattening. I flash an accusatory glance at Mom. Why does she do this? A small voice reminds me that I am in control of what I eat. The yummy cheese is there, but I don't have to eat it. I can totally ignore the yellow, shiny squares bristling with calories.

I begin piling up my plate with salad. I can have as much as I like of the green, bright pale leaves. Nobody is looking at me, as if I am not there. I know Mom still worries about me. She thinks I can't tell that she mentally counts every calorie passing my lips, hoping that I'll hit 1,000, and maybe even more. Today, she's not looking. The hopeful look has left her face. She's just staring at her plate and pushing what's on there from side to side. Nothing seems to be making it to her mouth. Is this a new strategy to get me to eat more? I can't decide.

I experiment by eating a small morsel of cheese. I quickly glance at my family. No one is watching. Maybe some new advice they got from my therapist? Quickly I gobble it up. The taste is exquisite, like little balloons of happiness bursting uncontrollably in my mouth. I can't stop. Steadily, I work my way through the entire plate of mouthful-sized cubes Mom has cut up in her precise way.

Soon after I have eaten the last bit, guilt overwhelms me. I feel fat. I probably look fat. Trying to mentally count the calories and assess the damage, I stare through the open window at the cherry tree in full bloom.

Everyone is quiet. Mom is still laboriously picking at her lunch, and Dad is wiping his eyes. He suffers from allergies this time of year. I take in the scene outside. Flowers, sprinklers, open windows—how can it be? Did Spring arrive last night? Is the overload of fat and calories making me delusional?

I try to concentrate and marshal my wandering thoughts. Other than the bizarre change of seasons, all looks familiar and as it should be. Through the kitchen door, I can see our family portrait, a favourite of mine. My slight frame is dwarfed by the bulging figures of Mom, Dad, and Ella.

I work hard to stay thin. Sometimes I do things in the bathroom I'd rather not talk about, but it's all worth it. I'm not there yet. There is still fat I need to shift. But I'm doing all the right things. At seventeen, I can still fit into the jeans I wore at my eighth birthday party. I lock eyes with the girl in the portrait and give her a wink. She stares back, sunken eyes, scrawny arms, limp hair…

"Mom, what happened to this picture? Look at me—I look sick!"

Mom stays silent, concentrating on her fork. Nobody looks up. Nobody says anything. Nothing at all.

As if I am not there.

ABOUT THE AUTHOR

Alexandra Filia was born and raised in Athens, Greece before moving to New York to complete her studies. There, she worked as a stockbroker, banker, and in professional publishing before selling everything and moving onto a boat. She's sailed the world writing about her adventures in a series of articles published in a cruising magazine. When she arrived in London on her boat *Nikia*, she founded and sold an award-winning business while raising two toddlers.

She and her partner share their home in London with her two amazing teenage daughters.

Alexandra has published three books in the Dream Series: *Love Is A Game: A Marriage Proposal in 90 Days*, *The Good Breakup: How to Get Him Back or Get over Him...for Good*, and *Forever Young: An Anti-Aging Guide for the Terrified*.